SEVEN DOORS TO SALVATION

A TALE OF DARKNESS AND LIGHT

JASKARAN CHAHAL

TABLE OF CONTENTS

PREFACE

Out of all the possible topics that I could've explored for my very first novel, I chose something that is genuinely important but often ignored, denied, and stigmatized in different parts of the world: mental health. Conversations about mental health are typically quiet and it's a subject that still fails to receive the proper attention it deserves. It's the foundation for this story and something that I've personally struggled to maintain as I've grown older.

We usually and incorrectly correlate people's moods with how they appear to us. If someone looks to be in shape or smiling at you, we generally assume that they're doing alright in their minds. The truth is that anyone's mental health can become vulnerable and quickly shift from day to day. Psychological and emotional well-being aren't easily measured as other things in our lives, which makes it more difficult to identify who's feeling broken and who's not.

The COVID-19 pandemic has only exacerbated the mental health crisis and as a result, people's emotions are as volatile as ever. It's no secret that anxiety, insecurity, and depression are steadily on the rise, particularly within younger generations. At this very moment, millions of people around the globe are suffering on the inside, trying to carry themselves with as much confidence and dignity as they can throughout an event that they could never have anticipated.

What you're about to read is essentially a self-help book under the veil of a fictional story. The character of Danny represents all of us who have struggled to uplift ourselves throughout our darkest moments. The setting of the Greater Toronto Area can be replaced with any location in the world that's relatable to you. Each unique chapter not only builds upon Danny's journey but is meant to get you thinking about your own situation and where your mental state stands. There are many pieces of advice and thoughtful lessons sprinkled throughout this story that are intended to promote a healthy mind, which you can apply to your life and use to improve your outlook.

If this book can become an outlet to help spread my message of optimism and hope to a larger audience, readers may realize that the light at the end of the tunnel is closer than it appears. Stories can contain the power to heal our internal wounds and provide therapy when it's most needed. If this story can change even one person's mindset by motivating them to remain positive throughout all the negativity that constantly surrounds us, then I'll have done my job.

Depression is one of most painful feelings you can ever experience in life but believe me, it can eventually be controlled and conquered. Looking back to when I first started this project, I'm grateful that I seized the opportunity to express my vision. Its potential to help other people far outweighs any of the initial doubts that I once had. I've poured my heart and soul into the words on these pages, so I humbly thank you for taking the time to read them. I hope that you'll not only enjoy this story but learn from it and pass its message on to others around you.

Jaskaran Chahal

THE WALK

I awaken with darkness surrounding me. My body is partially submerged in shallow water and it's aching as if I've fallen from the sky. I lay on my back and look up at the full moon that's providing the only source of light. The water gently moves forward and recedes back as I slowly lift my head off the ground. Where am I and what am I doing here? The panic slowly begins to set in, as none of this is familiar to me.

I struggle to regain my strength but force myself to expend as much of it as I can to move my body. I'm barely able to stand up. I take a few steps toward the shoreline before collapsing back down to the ground and plowing my head into sand. I'm out of breath like I've gotten the wind knocked out of me. As I'm down on my stomach, I move my head up and notice a swarm of trees in front of me. There's no sign of life anywhere.

Not only does everything hurt and I don't know how I got here, but something much worse has happened. For some reason, I can't remember anything besides my name. *Danny Singh* rings in my head. Beyond that, there's no other important information at all. I give myself a moment thinking that it's some sort of temporary amnesia. A few seconds of waiting later, my initial panic becomes amplified by a hundred. I have absolutely no memory about anything as if it's been totally wiped clean from my mind.

"Help!" I yell. My voice exits my throat in the raspiest condition.

I start to crawl further away from the water and closer to the trees. It appears to be a vast forest. I muster all the strength I have in me for my next attempt.

"IS THERE ANYONE OUT THERE!?" I scream, with as much oxygen as my lungs can afford to spare. Complete silence. I doubt I'll make it far if no one can hear me out here. I seem to be alone on this shore and my cries are going to waste.

I'm suddenly proven wrong as I hear a cracking noise coming from the direction of the forest. It sounds like twigs snapping under the weight of someone's footsteps. The closer they move to me, the louder they get.

"Hello? Is someone there?" I ask in a quieter tone, trying my best not to display any fear.

I keep my head raised out of caution and on a constant swivel. A few metres away, a hazy figure exits the forest. He looks around for the person who's been making all this noise. I quickly wipe my eyes with both of my knuckles to confirm I'm not hallucinating.

It's a man and he notices my body laying on the shore. He then approaches me with a slow and casual stride. His attire consists of black pants, black shoes, and a black full-sleeved shirt. The closer this figure moves to me, the more I'm able to clearly see his face. He appears to be much older than me with wrinkly skin, bags under his eyes, grey hair atop his head, and a grey beard decorating his face.

My eyes rapidly move down from his pale face to his waist as he pulls out a large knife with a black handle from his back pocket. It's sharp enough to harm me and my adrenaline rush instantly kicks in. I somehow manage to stand up on my feet again and I take some steps back away from the man. He continues to slowly move in my direction with his knife pointed right at me.

"Stay away from me! I'm warning you!" I yell. My hands are in the air and balled up into tight fists.

The man stops in his tracks and stares at me for a few seconds. He isn't afraid of me but more amused at my defensive state. I stand my ground, shaking and shivering but unwavering. The man opens his mouth to speak to me.

"It's alright," he says. "I'm not a threat to you."

Naturally, I don't take his words seriously at all and I stay planted in place with my fists in the air. I don't respond and I keep my attention solely focused on him in case he swings at me. He could attack at any second now but I'm not as vulnerable as he thinks I am.

To my surprise, the strange individual puts his knife back into his pocket and outstretches his hand instead.

"My name's Peri Gramer. I can help you get out of here," he says. He stands in his place intending to shake my hand.

I look around and cautiously survey my surroundings to see if there's anyone else out there waiting to get the jump on me. This must be his attempt to set a trap because he's realized he can't take me in a fight.

"Nice try, but I don't trust you. What kind of a name is Peri? Did you just make that up?" I ask. I turn my head toward the trees and then back at him. "I'm not scared of you. I'll take you all on!"

"There's no one else out there," the man says with his hand still outstretched. "What's your name?" he asks.

"My name's none of your business. And I totally believe you," I say, nodding my head.

"Believe me, it's only us. You're surely not afraid of a frail old man like me?" he teases. "I apologize for the knife. It was only to protect myself if I really needed to… What's your name?"

This man isn't budging, and he doesn't seem to be an immediate threat anymore. I could be wrong and regret it later. I lower my guard and I slowly approach him. I outstretch my right hand toward him while my left hand is ready to swing at his face if I need to. I shake his hand while looking right into his eyes and he does the same to me.

"Danny Singh," I say, firmly gripping his hand before letting go. I'm trying my best not to look or sound too defenceless.

My brain feels like it's covered in dense clouds, and I still have no idea about what's going on or where I am. I'm continuously questioning if I'm in any real danger and if I should risk everything by running away. For now, I'll take my chances and ask this *Peri* person about what he knows instead.

"Where are we? I don't see any roads, buildings, or people anywhere. How do we get out of here?" I ask.

"Oh, none of those belong here. The only way out, is *in*," he says. He nods his head in the direction of the forest from where he emerged.

"What are you talking about? What's in there?" I ask. I stare into the darkness of the forest in front of us. It doesn't seem to be the most welcoming of places.

"The answer to all your questions and the only way to retrieve your missing memories," Peri replies.

How does he know about that? He must've had something to do with this!

"What did you do to me?" I ask. "Why can't I remember anything?"

"Don't worry, *Danny*. All will be revealed to you if you take a leap of faith and trust me," Peri says. "If you refuse, you can stay here on this shore but no one else will come to help you."

His offer doesn't sound too promising, and I freeze up instead of speaking any further. I try to consider all possible scenarios of what I could do next, from taking Peri's knife away from him, to running into the forest myself, or moving along this shoreline in hopes of encountering someone else. None of the strategies in my head seem sensible enough to pull off. Peri begins to walk ahead of me as I remain standing in place.

"Are you coming?" Peri asks, standing a few steps away from the tip of the forest.

I cautiously look around me and then downward. I'm wearing a dark grey t-shirt, black shoes, and blue jeans, which I pat down to check all my pockets. I pull out a cellphone and a car key. The cellphone doesn't turn on, as I view my dim and pale reflection in the black screen made of glass.

Dark black hair covers my head, and a stubble beard outlines my cheeks. My eyes look extremely tired, as if I haven't slept in days. The car key is useless to me because I don't see any vehicle or parking lot around. I'm also wearing a vintage watch around my left wrist, with a white face, silver hands, and a brown leather strap. I turn the dial and shake it around but it's not in working condition, as all three of its hands are stuck at the number six.

Besides that, I have nothing else of value or anything that could provide a single clue as to what's going on. There's no one else to follow and nowhere else to go. I guess I have no choice but to follow this man and take his word for the time being.

"Alright, I'll come with you," I say.

Peri looks pleased and smiles, waiting for me to walk forward and catch up to him. My body isn't hurting as much as it was when I first awoke. All that adrenaline must've played a role in waking me up from my dormant state and breathing a little life back into me.

The full moon continues to illuminate the night sky and there is a sense of mysterious beauty around it. Peri and I make it off the shore and as we enter the dark forest, the bright moonlight becomes covered by thick branches and leaves. I still feel like I'm going to be ambushed at any moment, so I stay alert with my eyes monitoring my surroundings.

The further we venture into this dark forest, the dimmer the moonlight is with each step. There's nothing of interest that crosses our path until I eventually see something far away in the distance, past hundreds of trees. It seems to be a small and thick white wall from what my eyes can tell. There also seems to be a faint noise coming from above it but it's hardly audible from where we are.

"What's that?" Over there," I say while pointing it out to Peri, who then looks in that direction.

"I wouldn't advise going there," he says.

"I'm not going to run off now if that's what you mean. Is there even a main road or a town close by here?" I ask.

"No roads or towns, only forest and water," Peri replies. I doubt the validity of his statement.

"What are you doing here anyway? What's your role in all this?" I ask. Peri doesn't reply and keeps walking. I'm annoyed and I need answers, so I ask him again in a louder tone. "I asked *you* what you're doing *here?*"

Peri sighs. "This isn't about me, it's about you. *You* don't belong here, so it's *my* responsibility to help you get out before it's too late," he says.

"I have no idea what your riddles mean. What do you mean *before it's too late?*" I ask.

Peri doesn't reply and continues to face forward as he's walking. All I want to know is what's going on, but I feel like I'm talking to a wall. I keep trying to think about how I arrived here but the only thing I can remember is my name and waking up in the water. There's no recollection of anything prior to that.

We continue our walk through this maze of a forest. Just when the minutes are starting to feel like hours, Peri finally stops and turns around to face me. There's something unusual behind him that I catch a brief glimpse of before he covers my view. It looked like an empty area with a bunch of wooden blocks in the middle.

"What's behind me isn't going to make much sense to you right away. I know you'll have more questions than answers, but try not to overthink it," Peri starts.

I'm already not liking the sound of this.

"You're going to see seven doors lined up next to each other. Your task is to simply open and walk through each of them, one at a time," Peri says.

He was right, as I have a million more questions now. Peri notices the visible confusion on my face and as I'm about to make a comment, he prevents me from doing so.

"Please, just listen for now. Once you've walked through each door, all your memories will be returned to you and you'll be able to leave this place."

I remain silent and begin to think that I must've really lost my mind. This has got to be the weirdest dream I've ever had but I know that I'll wake up at any moment now. There's no way that any of this could be real. I hold my right arm out in front of me and pinch my wrist with my left hand. I feel a slight tingling pain. I then slap myself on my right cheek, hoping to end all this and wake up. Again, I feel a sharp pain on my face but nothing else happens. Peri watches me make a fool out of myself before speaking again.

"Do you understand what you have to do?" he asks.

"I need to see what you're talking about because whatever you're telling me sounds like total nonsense," I say.

"Very well," Peri says as he steps out of my way. I move up and notice what appears to be a circular clearing in the middle of this forest, where the moonlight is shining brightly once more. There are leaves on the ground, but no dense trees are present within this decent size of an area. Right in the centre of it are those same wooden blocks that I saw a moment ago. They are indeed wooden doors inserted into wooden doorframes. A total of seven of them are standing in a line, side-by-side. I walk into the middle of this clearing to inspect what this absurdity is all about. I view both sides of the doors and there's nothing in front of them or behind them. This is the definition of lunacy.

"I don't get it. There's nothing even behind them," I say. "What am I supposed to walk in to?" I step around them again to check if this is some sort of trap. They're nothing but simple pieces of wood with brass doorknobs attached to them. "This has to be a joke," I say, followed with a chuckle. I must be going mad.

"Once you open the first door and set foot inside, you'll understand," Peri replies. "These doors were made for you and you alone."

What does he mean *made for me?* Before I bombard Peri with questions, the first door in the line of seven begins to display a subtle glow all around it.

"You're on the clock now. The sooner you leave this place, the better," Peri says.

"Really? No kidding!" I reply.

Peri directs his arms to the door furthest to our left that's glowing. I'm assuming this is where I'm supposed to start. Out of a little curiosity and revolt, I try to open the second door instead. The doorknob doesn't budge at all, no matter how much force I use on it. I go from grasping it with one hand to using both of my hands, but still no luck. There's probably a lock attached to it. I then try to kick the door down with all my might. My leg ends up experiencing pain as the door simply doesn't budge. I try to open the other five remaining doors by turning their knobs and it's the same result for all of them. None of my attempts are working and I'm only making a fool out of myself again. This has to be some kind of a trick.

"What are these doors made of?" I ask. I take a few steps back to view them all in line. Peri doesn't say anything and directs my attention to the first door again.

"You have to start from the first door and make your way through the line. There's no other way," Peri says.

I guess I really do have to start from the beginning.

I walk over to the first door and glare at this seemingly harmless, rectangular piece of ordinary wood. The subtle glow around this door makes it appear simple and strange at the same time. I continue to tell myself that this is all one big dream and I'll eventually wake up from it. Until then, I'll play this little game to pass the time. My right hand reaches out and holds on to the brass doorknob.

"Good luck Danny," Peri says.

"Sure," I reply.

I begin to turn the knob of the first door in a clockwise motion. I then slowly push it outward as the hinges of the doorframe allow the door to move. As the door is opening, my mouth is agape and I squint my eyes because I know this can't be possible. Last I checked, there was nothing behind this door from the outside. Now, inside of the door is a different story. It contains total darkness within it, resembling a black void.

How can this be? This is most definitely a dream.

I take a deep breath and try not to show any signs of weakness to Peri. Once the door opens all the way, I take a few steps inside of its frame.

The darkness begins to engulf me from every direction. I swiftly turn around and see Peri following me in before he closes the door behind him. The trees, the night sky, and the only source of light from the moon completely disappear after he does so. I have absolutely no awareness of my surroundings and it's as if I'm being sucked into a cold black hole with no escape. I'm more fearful in this moment than I was on the shore. What have I gotten myself into?

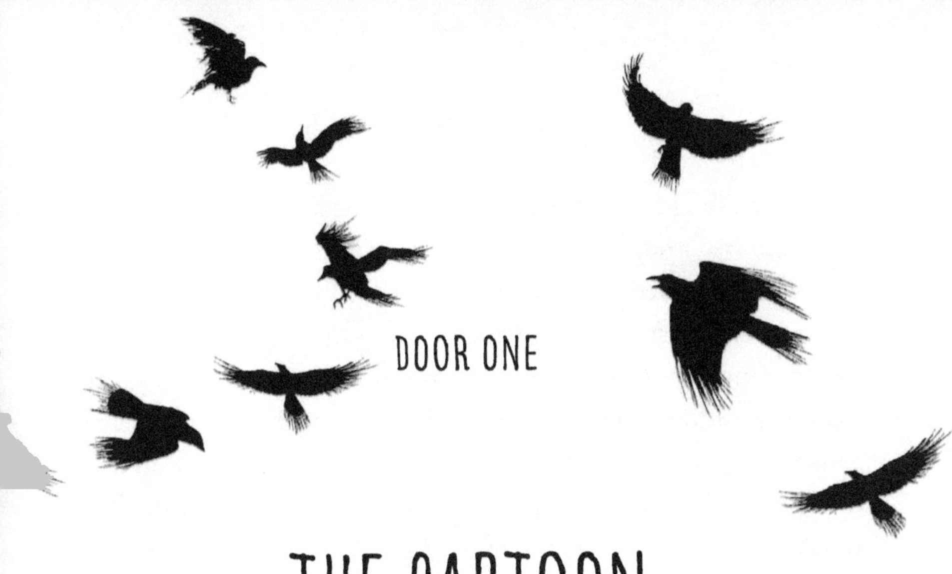

THE CARTOON

"Peri!?" I yell, turning in every direction and assuming I've gone blind. I can't see anything within this pitch-black darkness, not even my own hands in front of my face. I feel cold as if frost is forming all over me.

Suddenly, a glimmering white substance made up of individual floating flecks begins to appear in front of me. It hovers and shines in front of my eyes, which also helps illuminate the surrounding darkness.

More of this substance begins to show up and it's getting brighter by the second. There must be millions of these tiny shining flecks freely swaying around, as if they have a mind of their own.

As I raise my hand to touch them, the flecks scatter and rapidly fly outward in every direction. They're in front of me, behind me, beside me, below me, and above me. Once they reach a specific area, they stop in their tracks as if they're trying to mold something in three dimensions.

As this mysterious substance is working away in the background, I hold my right arm out in front of me and I jump from the sudden shock. There's no weight to my arm and I'm somehow able to see right through it. I begin swinging it up and down, then left and right. As I'm quickly moving my arm, Peri walks over and I drop it to stare at him. This isn't how he looked in the forest at all, now resembling a translucent ghost.

"No way. What kind of sorcery is this?" I ask. I'm horrified and intrigued at the same time.

"You'll get used to it eventually," Peri replies.

The glimmering substance is still flowing around us and taking the form of various items. It looks as if it's transitioning from a free-flowing liquid to tangible solids, like water freezing in an ice tray. I begin to recognize certain objects that are being formed by this flexible entity. Among other things, I recognize a television and some furniture that's taken shape in front of me. These white flecks seem to be constructing an environment around me and Peri. I couldn't possibly be more confused than I am now.

"What is this place? And who are you really?" I ask while slightly trembling.

"You'll see in a few short moments, and I already told you who I am. My name's Peri and I'm here to help you through this," he says. "Try to be patient."

"How is any of this supposed to help me get back to where I came from? It feels like I'm getting even more lost than I already was."

Peri doesn't say anything and displays a smile instead. I doubt he's going to relay any more information for now, so I keep quiet and continue observing this strange phenomenon.

The environment around us seems to be almost completed. Peri and I wait as the process finalizes and the last few flecks are moving to attach themselves to a nearby object.

A few seconds later, the glimmering white substance remains completely still as everything seems to be set in place. All the various items and objects have become solidified within the environment that's been created for us.

As if that weren't enough of a display, the millions of white flecks then fill up with a spectrum of vivid colours. It's a gigantic, interactive, three-dimensional painting that's been brought to life and we're standing right in the middle of it. Although I have no memory of anything, I'm certain that there's no such element in the world that can function like these glimmering flecks.

Peri and I seem to be standing in the corner of someone's living room. Nothing in my mind gives me the slightest idea of what any of this could mean. I have no memory of this place. I analyze our surroundings to take a closer look. There's beige carpet beneath our shoes, along with a brown couch on our right, an old boxy television set to our left, a window behind us, and an open doorway a few paces in front of us.

"What is this?" I ask.

"Your journey back has officially begun," Peri replies.

"What's that supposed to mean?" I ask again.

Before Peri responds, a young boy casually walks into the living room from the open doorway in front of us. He's wearing dark grey sweatpants and a blue t-shirt, while holding a cereal bowl in his hands. He walks toward the couch and plops himself down on it. The boy then scoops some cereal with his spoon and puts it in his mouth.

I'm still standing in place wondering about what's going on, what we're doing here, and who we're looking at.

The young boy picks up a remote control and turns the television on. He flips through a few channels before settling on one that's showing cartoon characters. He raises the volume by a tiny amount and begins to watch while munching away on his cereal.

From the corner of the room, I start waving my arm up and down to check if this boy will notice anything from his peripheral vision. He doesn't seem to budge and continues watching the cartoon show, totally unaware of me and Peri standing in the same room as him.

"Can't he see us?" I ask.

"Nope. He can't see, hear, or feel us in any way. We're invisible to him," Peri responds.

Out of curiosity, I walk over to the young boy and stand directly in front of him, attempting to block his sight of the television. Once again, he doesn't budge and looks right through me. At this point, I'm convinced that he doesn't know we're here.

I decide to sit next to him on the couch and feel its material with my hands. I can feel the soft fabric running through my fingers, but I know that it isn't real as I witnessed it being created in front of me.

Everything around me displays a very subtle white aura around it, like an odd ghostly environment, but it's only noticeable when

I stare at it for too long. Besides that, it's as if I've been transported to some other place that feels identical to reality.

I turn my head toward the boy and lean in to take a closer look at him. He has dark black hair, dark brown eyes, and tan skin like me. I lean back and face the television.

"So now what? We watch cartoons with this kid and enjoy our day?" I ask.

"For now," Peri responds.

There's something eerie about this place. I feel as if I should know where we are, but my mind keeps drawing a blank every time I try to think about my past.

"Why can't I remember anything?" I ask.

"Give it some time," Peri replies.

Peri's answers are good for nothing at this point so I sit, watch, and wait.

The young boy occasionally smiles whenever something funny happens in the cartoon. There's a black cat that climbs a huge tree and attempts to traverse along a long branch to eat a small yellow bird. Before it's able to do so, the bird cleverly outwits the cat and cuts the tree branch off with a saw. The cat ends up falling a long way down to the ground, which makes the young boy beside me express a small chuckle.

It seems that the boy wants to keep the noise down to a minimum. Every time something funny happens in the cartoon, it's the same result. It's not open or loud laughter but instead, softened and held back.

I wonder if anyone else may be in the house. I get up from the couch and walk around the living room. I notice a small picture that's framed and hung up on the wall beside the entrance. It appears to be of the same young boy as a toddler, in between what seems like his parents. From the surface, it looks like a decent household with a loving family.

Outside this living room, there's a staircase and a narrow hallway leading to a small kitchen. It's not a luxurious mansion by any standards, but probably big enough for this small family of three.

I look back at the young boy, trying to get an idea of what any of this could mean for me. Why am I being showed something so irrelevant to my current situation?

The boy turns his attention away from the television for a moment and stares out to the window on his left.

I walk toward it to get a glimpse at what he could be looking at. It's a sunny day outside with the trees gently swaying with the wind. I see a few houses down the road, all small in their size and most likely similar to the one I'm currently standing in. I can see this house's driveway with an old car parked on it.

The boy lets out a brief sigh before turning his attention back to the cartoon.

Maybe he wants to be somewhere else, but he's stuck inside? I can't figure out the context and I have no idea how to decipher any of this. I give up trying to solve this puzzle and I fall back to my seat on the couch.

"Peri you gotta give me something… None of this is making any sense to me," I say.

Before Peri has a chance to say anything, a loud and aggressive voice booms throughout the environment.

"OY! WHERE ARE YOU?" a man shouts as he assertively walks down the staircase outside of the living room. Each step he takes creaks under his weight.

"I'm right here dad, in the TV room," the boy responds.

The boy's dad enters the room as if he's about to stumble at any moment. He's not walking in a normal fashion, constantly swinging from side to side. He's wearing a white tank top and light grey sweatpants.

"What are you doing watching cartoons? Did you finish your homework?" the dad asks.

"The good ones only come on Saturday mornings. And yeah dad, I finished it last night," the boy says.

"What about studying or doing your chores around the house? Why aren't those done?" the dad asks.

"I was going to do them later," the boy replies with his head down.

"When is later? Two hours from now? Six hours from now?" the dad asks.

"Just after this show finishes," the boy says.

I walk right up to this arrogant man to see what his problem is. He's clearly drunk as his eyes are bloodshot red and his breath reeks of alcohol. There's something familiar about him though, as if I know him from somewhere.

The man abruptly walks right through me and approaches the television. I turn around and observe him aggressively push a button to turn it off. For a brief second, the boy looks up at the black screen with innocent eyes before putting his head back down.

"There you go. The show is finished now!" the dad says. "Wash all the dishes and vacuum the house. Once you're done, I want the lawn mowed. Both yards, front and back. Get to work."

"Okay," the boy somberly replies. He doesn't try to fight back at all.

The man acknowledges the boy's presence with one last condescending sneer and walks out of the room while wobbling.

Witnessing this interaction triggers something strange within my mind. I stagger and fall backward on the couch. I feel an overwhelming sensation in my head that I haven't experienced so far. My mind feels like it's on fire as I'm beginning to remember bits and pieces of my early life.

"What's happening to me?" I ask Peri.

"Some of your memories are being restored to you. Sit tight," Peri says.

I close my eyes and let whatever's happening run its course. I somehow begin remembering the earliest parts of my childhood and my upbringing.

Peri didn't bring me to some random living room to watch cartoons with an unknown boy. This was once *my* living room, and the little boy is *me*! The man who was creating a ruckus in front of us is none other than my own dad. Whatever's happening in my mind is crazy on all levels and simply inexplicable.

"This is a memory from my childhood," I say. "Why'd you bring me here?"

"This is one of the first times in your life when you began to feel a sense of hopelessness," Peri replies.

Peri's not lying as my mind takes it one step further. I begin to *feel* the same range of emotions that the boy is feeling in this exact moment in time. He's still sitting next to me on the couch and I look at him from a different perspective this time around. It's hard to believe that this was once me, but there I am. It's like I'm staring into a mirror that's reflecting my younger self.

What do I even call him? Younger Me? Past Me? Little Danny? To avoid overthinking and confusing myself any further, I'll stick to calling this reflection my *past self*… or better yet, "*Past Danny.*"

Past Danny lets out a gentle sigh. I can feel his excitement being drained because all he wanted to do was watch cartoons on his Saturday morning. He finishes the remaining cereal in his bowl before getting up from the couch. He then slowly walks to the exit of the living room, accepting his orders made by his dad.

"Why didn't I remember anything or experience these emotions as soon as we arrived in this room?" I ask Peri as I'm curious about the long delay in between.

"A specific event has to be triggered for your memories to be unlocked and restored back to you. In this case, it was right after your dad turned the TV off and told you to get to work," Peri explains.

I anxiously look around, thinking about how I don't belong here and how I need to escape more than ever. My right leg beings to quiver but I keep it subtle enough so that Peri doesn't notice. I don't understand what's happening and I feel frightened.

Peri notices my agitation once my constant shaking isn't so subtle anymore. "I know this is a lot to take in right now," he says. "Take some time to regain your composure and reflect on the memories you've just recovered. It'll help you calm down. I'll be here until then."

I don't say anything but instead, decide to listen to him and follow his advice. I lean back on the couch and close my eyes. I attempt to remember as much of my life as I possibly can, starting from the very beginning.

I was born on August 13th and raised in the city of Brampton, which was a decent place within Canada that had everything I ever needed close by.

I try not to ponder too much about the technical details. I need to focus more on myself to remember who I was and who I am as a person.

I remember growing up in this very household, which wasn't the greatest of experiences and far from perfect. My dad was a drunkard who drove a delivery truck during the day while my mom worked the afternoon shift in a factory that produced refined wood. She would often work overtime on Saturday mornings, which may explain why she wasn't present in the memory that played out in front of me.

From Monday to Friday, I went to school during the day and struggled to make any good friends. In the afternoons, I came home and struggled to have a friendly conversation with my dad. I always felt like I couldn't approach him or talk to him about anything openly and comfortably.

I was also an only child, which didn't help because I had no siblings to socialize with, fight with, or have fun with. When I was really young, I remember asking my mom about why I couldn't have a sibling. She sat me down to have a lengthy conversation, explaining that her body wouldn't allow for her to have any more kids. My mom was an only child herself, so she knew exactly what I was going through. She never wanted me to feel alone in the house because that's how she felt when she was growing up.

The times I wished for a sibling the most were whenever my dad went out of his way to pick on me. Alcohol was my dad's best friend and it turned him into the devil whenever he'd consume it. He would find solace in doing or saying things that agitated me whenever he had the chance. When my mom was at work in the afternoons, I didn't have anyone to stand up for me but myself. Both of my parents lost their own parents when they were teenagers, so I wasn't lucky enough to grow up with any overly protective grandparents either.

My dad's alcohol addiction ruined many of his relations with friends, cousins, coworkers, and even his older brother. I never met this estranged uncle because he and his family cut ties with my dad before I was born. My mom told me that it was a quarrel over the division of ancestral property after their parents passed away. A dispute over a few acres of land turned blood brothers into complete strangers. After all these relationships were destroyed forever, it's as if my dad made it his mission to ruin my relationship with him too.

While I was a student in elementary school, I was oblivious to how my dad treated me. I assumed it was normal behaviour that existed within every household. I didn't know any better because I was so young. It wasn't until middle school when I started to realize that my dad never treated me with the respect or love that I deserved.

My classmates would tell me stories of what they did on the weekends with their own dads, from going to amusement parks and hiking on nature trails to learning how to use a computer. I couldn't relate to any of it and that's when I started to feel the hurtful impact of what I'd been missing out on all along.

From what I can recall, this memory in the living room that Peri and I observed probably took place when I was about 12 years old. I was in middle school and that was around the time my dad started pushing me to mow the lawn, especially when all the other kids on my street were playing basketball in their driveways.

It's not that I had an issue with the chores he assigned me. The real issues arose whenever I did them too late, did them incorrectly, or even if I did them correctly and they weren't up to my dad's high standards. He would make me do them repeatedly until they were done exactly the way he wanted them done. As I was almost a teenager at that point, there were a few times when I rebelled by talking back to my dad. I felt the whip and sting of his leather belt on my body soon after.

For some reason, my dad was always angry and fed up with his life. He must've thought that the only way to get through it was with the help of a bottle, as well as projecting all his problems on to me and my mom. I always tried to take the brunt of his wrath in my attempt to protect her.

I had heard of parents being strict to teach their kids genuine lessons about discipline, but what my dad used to do to me was more in line with unnecessary and cruel punishments. I remember the time when he was once so drunk that he picked me up and threw me at the couch for his amusement. I was a little kid then, maybe only six or seven years old at the time. I bounced right off the couch and landed hard on the carpet below. I got up and pretended not to be hurt so that my dad would view me as strong. I pathetically viewed many similar events like this one as "tough love."

Realistically, the lack of any real love from my dad, combined with all the physical and mental abuse, resulted in a disaster of a childhood for me. It slowly contributed toward developing insecurity and anxiety within me, even though I didn't know what any of these things were back then.

As a child, I thought that I had to respect my dad no matter what because he was one of my parents. When I turned 13, I abandoned that philosophy altogether. While I still listened to him because I was living in his house, I no longer respected him or viewed him as anything close to a confidant in my life.

I remember trying to enjoy my time at school during the day as much as I could. I found comfort in focusing on my classes and I paid close attention to my teachers whenever they spoke. I didn't have anything else to look forward to once it was time to go home, so I signed up for different sports teams and clubs after school. I did whatever it took to avoid my dad's presence. Although I didn't make any close friends, I consistently achieved good grades and participated in many extracurricular activities. None of it seemed to matter at the end of the day though, as I considered myself to be a loser from a social standpoint.

I remember I used to dread Fridays the most, as all the students in my classes were thrilled for the weekend and would announce their plans out loud. I never had anything special to share, especially whenever I knew my mom would be busy the next morning to work overtime and I'd be stuck at home with my dad for the first half of the day. I couldn't even watch a few cartoons on a Saturday morning because my dad treated me like I was committing a sin that had to be cleansed with rigorous chores.

I try remembering my life beyond my middle school years but I'm unable to do so. I can only remember everything up until my graduation ceremony. I try a few more times before acknowledging that it's simply not possible right now. Any memories after that period become hazy, clouded, and censored. Everything ahead of the eighth grade is seemingly locked away behind a vault and I don't have the key to access it.

Once I've finished recollecting my thoughts, I finally open my eyes and look around the room. This was the very "home" that I grew up in, a word that I used more when I was young. Later on, it resembled a prison that kept me from having any fun in my life.

I feel chills thinking about how much I had to endure as a young boy compared to all the other kids around me. I turn my attention toward Peri, who's still standing by the window with his back against the wall and waiting for me to speak.

"I remember my childhood and early teenage years, but I can't remember anything past middle school," I say.

"It's a good start. Don't worry about the rest for now. All will be revealed in due time," Peri replies. "One at a time, piece by piece."

Peri speaks as if he's planned all this in advance and knows what to expect. His occasional comments and statements are more like riddles. I attempt to gauge him a bit more. "I feel like crap on the inside so if that's what you wanted, I hope you're happy."

"No Danny. This isn't what I want for you but it's something that needs to be done. Whatever you're experiencing right now may make you feel down, but it's progress," Peri says.

I'm not sure about what he means by that, but witnessing this memory play out and experiencing the same emotions from my past self gave me a piece of my mind back. That's definitely some progress in my books.

When I was back in the forest and had a blank slate in my head, I didn't feel any emotions as I do now. As soon as I somehow became linked with my past self and recovered these specific memories, it was like my mind found some long-lost treasure. On the downside, I now have an immense concentration of negativity within my mind that I can't seem to get rid of. It's a resentful feeling toward my dad more than anything else. It feels like a spider web that's stuck to me and can't easily be shaken off.

What Peri mentioned before was true. I do feel a sense of hopelessness now, along with other sentiments of disappointment, anger, and grief. When I was at that age, I only wanted a normal childhood.

Isn't that what all children expect to have? Unconditional love from their parents and good memories to cherish for the rest of their lives? It sounds simple in theory, but it's a not a life that every child is lucky enough to live. Either way, if this is the price that I have to pay in order to continue and successfully restore my entire memory, I accept these conditions.

I get up from the couch and begin to pace around in circles as my mind tries to cope with what's going on.

"We don't get to choose who our parents are," Peri says. "Some are good, some are bad, and some are both. You didn't deserve the dad that you got, but he helped mold you into the better person you are now, whether you want to accept it or not."

I should already understand this concept, but I allow Peri to continue. For some reason, I feel reassured knowing someone else can mildly understand me and relate to what I've been through.

"I'm sorry you had to go through all of that with a person who should've been your role model," Peri says.

I freeze up because this seems like the very first time that I'm hearing anyone mention these words out loud to me, and that too from a total stranger. I try to play it cool and act unbothered, but I feel much better after hearing Peri's words.

"It's okay, it is what it is. I stopped wishing for things to be different a long time ago when I realized they would never change," I say.

"I want you to remember something," Peri says. "Things *do* eventually change for the better. Sometimes it happens right away and other times it takes longer than expected. Now of course when you're a young boy, it's tough. Everything seems to be out of your control, and you depend on your parents for everything. But there's sprinkles of happiness to be found in between, even if you think there's not."

"My dad never made me happy from what I remember. He was nothing but an abusive alcoholic who always made me feel guilty like I did something wrong. I don't know why I'm telling you this but, on some nights when he was crazier than usual, I used to pray that he wouldn't wake up the next morning," I say. "Who wishes that for their own dad of all people? For the longest time, my life was pretty much a nightmare without no escape. Where were these bits of 'happiness' that you're talking about?" I ask.

"I understand your frustration, but your childhood wasn't completely all doom and gloom. There were good times as well Danny," Peri says.

My mood changes from being somewhat calm to feeling a sudden surge of anger pulsing throughout me. However, this time it's not toward my dad, but at Peri after the comment he's just made.

"How could you possibly know that and who are you to tell me any of this anyway?" I shout at Peri. "What good is a childhood when your own dad never bothered to get you a single birthday cake, gift, or take you out to go trick-or-treating? Actually, forget that small stuff and let me rephrase it better. What good is a life when your own dad prioritizes his booze over his own boy? How could you possibly know the answer to that?"

Peri pauses for a few moments, which seems like another one of his attempts to calm me down. It ends up working and I let out a sigh of frustration.

"I've seen the road ahead of you and I'm here to show it to you," Peri says. "There are good times ahead that follow these bad times, even if you think there's not. Whenever we fall down, the only thing left for us to do is rise up again. I need you to try to control these volatile emotions you're feeling. I need you to work with me, not against me. As long as you can do that, I can help you get your entire memory back and leave this place."

Peri extends his hand as if it's a peace offering. I look at it for a few seconds and think about how I have no other option but to trust this old man. If he's truly the only one who can help me through this ordeal, I'll follow his lead.

I extend my hand to shake Peri's.

"I'm sorry, I didn't mean to burst out like that. This was a sensitive time for me. Seeing my past self like that brought back all these painful emotions and man… Please, just help me get out of here," I say.

"I apologize as well. I should've worded what I was saying in a better way," Peri says. "I think we've spent enough time here in your old living room. I'd like to take you to a more positive time if you're ready to move on."

"I'm ready, let's go," I respond quickly. "I hope I never have to set foot in this place ever again."

"Very well," Peri says. He closes his eyes and raises his right hand out in front of him. Peri's fingers are in a formation like he's either about to snap them or cast some sort of magic spell. I doubt anything else could surprise me at this point.

Before he does anything, I take one last glance around this living room. I happen to look outside of the window, and I see a car pulling up in the driveway that I recognize.

"No wait! That's my-"

Before I'm able to finish my sentence and say "mom," Peri snaps his fingers and something incomprehensible begins to happen once again. The environment around us instantly breaks apart, disintegrating back into its unmolded and free-flowing state again. The illusion from this realistic memory is finally broken and I realize how absorbed I was within its life-like appearance.

We're standing back in the dark void that we were in before my old living room was formed, but not for long. The same tiny flecks begin to form another environment around us. Whatever this glimmering white substance is made of, it has to be from some other world. They shoot outward in every direction again, creating more various objects in the utmost intricate details.

"What is this stuff?" I ask Peri. "Can it replicate anything?"

"It's made of an element that's not on the periodic table if that's what you're asking. And oh yes, it can take the shape of something as small as an atom to an area as big as an entire city," Peri says.

I still feel like this is all a dream because there's no other way that any of this is remotely possible. I stare in awe as the white glimmering flecks are replicating an environment that appears to be much larger than the living room. I decide to name this weird and magical substance *"glimmer,"* to keep things as simple as I can with all that's going on in my mind.

Once the glimmer has stopped moving and the environment has become solidified, it fills up with vivid colours again. It truly feels indistinguishable from reality. The very first thing that I notice are bright flashing lights everywhere, along with the sound of games.

Peri and I seem to be standing in the middle of an arcade, with a plethora of activities and loud noises all around us. I walk around to get a feel for our new surrounding. I see children of all ages excitedly running around and playing game after game.

"Again, you're sure that no one can see us or feel us?" I ask. It's like I'm trying to confirm the parameters of my madness.

"Yes, I'm sure," Peri says. He stretches his arm out in front of an incoming kid's face, who's running down the same aisle we're standing in. The kid runs right though Peri's invisible arm and doesn't flinch at all. That'll do it for me.

This arcade has everything, from retro pinball machines to whack-a-mole and racing games with seats and steering wheels. This has to be every kid's ideal destination away from home. The atmosphere is entirely different from my old living room as this place is so vibrant and everyone is so energetic.

"Why are we here?" I ask.

"You'll see in a moment. Better yet, you'll *feel* it," Peri says.

This place is huge, and it makes my living room look like a tiny cubicle. Peri wasn't messing around when he said that the glimmer is able to replicate much bigger environments.

We continue to walk throughout the open spaces and aisles, viewing what everyone's doing. A young girl wins prize tickets from a wheel-spinning game to my right and she's ecstatic to share the news with her friends. Meanwhile on my left, a young boy loses a gruesome fighting game against his friend as the screen says "fatality." He frowns and stomps away to go play another game.

There's so many things happening all at once that it starts to become overwhelming. It's quite a departure from my mundane and dull living room.

Peri and I keep walking throughout this arena of entertainment until we turn a corner and I eventually stop in place. A few metres out in front of me, there's a woman standing by a young teenage boy, who's shooting little basketballs into a net that's moving from side to side. They're both wearing blue jeans and matching black t-shirts with cartoon graphics on them. I can't see their faces because they're focused on the game, so I decide to move closer.

For some reason, I think I may be looking at myself. While I couldn't wrap my head around what was happening in the previous memory, I feel like I'm better equipped now. I choose not to question my gut instinct and I follow through with it.

I don't say anything to Peri or ask any questions this time. I take some steps forward until I'm in range and start to hear their voices.

"I need 10 more and only have 20 seconds left!" the boy shouts as he's shooting as many basketballs as he can. There's a small screen above the hoop that displays an animated basketball player who's counting down the seconds until the game is over. The boy gives it his all with maximum determination.

10…9…8…7… the seconds tick down.

"Go, go, go!" the woman beside him cheers on with excitement.

The boy needs one more shot to go in before he wins the game. There's three seconds left on the timer. He misses his first attempt, but he quickly collects another ball that rolls down the sloped surface and chucks it upward at the very last second. The ball goes into the net just in time before the buzzer goes off.

"YES! I GOT IT!" he shouts while jumping up and down with his arms in the air. He turns to face the woman with a huge grin on his face.

"Yay! High five, Danny!" the woman says, before the boy jumps up to connect with her outstretched hand.

As soon as I see both of their faces and hear her call me Danny, I stagger to the side as Peri holds me up with one arm. I begin to feel the same strange phenomenon I experienced in my living room with my dad. I inherit the exact same emotions my past self is currently experiencing right in front of me with my mom.

I feel so much different now, the opposite of how I was feeling after my dad scolded me for watching television. Happiness, excitement, satisfaction, and enthusiasm are some of the many feelings swirling around in my mind now. More of my former memories have also been restored and it feels like another piece of the puzzle has been filled in.

"That's me and my mom!" I say while smiling and continuously staring at the two individuals in front of me.

"It is, and it looks like you were quite the basketball star," Peri says. He's still holding on to me and making sure I don't fall down.

When all these memories come back to me, they hit my mind all at once and it's difficult to process. It feels like a load of heavy bricks unexpectedly drop on top of my head.

Peri and I continue to walk behind my past self and my mom as they approach a food court. I'm feeling pure bliss in this moment and my smile doesn't disappear for a second. I'm so happy to be able to see my mom again, even if all this still seems to be a dream and far from any sense of reality.

"Let's take a seat," Peri says.

We approach a table with two empty chairs and sit down. Meanwhile, Past Danny and my mom are standing in line to order some food. It appears to be a burger joint, and my past self is pointing at various items on the massive menu above.

"So, what do you remember now?" Peri asks.

"I remember that we went here on my birthday, August 13th. It was before high school started in a few weeks," I say. I also remember that I didn't have any close friends to celebrate my birthday with, but I intentionally leave this information out so I don't embarrass myself.

"A day before this, I had a huge argument with my dad. My mom knew how upset I was, and she didn't want me to be alone on my birthday. She called in sick for work the next day so that she could take me out on a weekday afternoon," I say.

"She seems like a very nice lady," Peri says. "I had mentioned that there were good times in your life. This is one of them."

I start to understand what Peri was previously implying in the living room. I was being arrogant and didn't want to listen to him, but the emotions I'm currently experiencing are making me believe that everything is alright in my world.

I feel euphoric and realize how special this memory is as it's playing out in front of me. Past Danny and my mom receive their food and find a table to sit at. They're each carrying one tray with a burger sitting on top of it, along with a side of fries and a soft drink. They sit down a few tables away from us and I can see the anticipation on their faces as they unwrap their meals.

My mom always did the most to put a smile on my face. Not only did she know that I had no one else to celebrate my birthday with, but she also knew that I was nervous about starting high school in a few weeks.

Taking a day off work doesn't seem like a big deal, but it meant the world to me. Not having her around in the afternoons from Monday to Friday was difficult because I was forced to see my dad more than her.

Every Friday evening, I used to pray that she wouldn't work an overtime shift the next morning. I understood our family's financial situation and knew that we could use the extra money, but I still wanted her to spend time with me instead. Whenever my wish came true and my mom didn't go to work, that's when our house felt like a home to me. It made all the difference and I remember feeling so comforted knowing I'd have her there to talk to.

When you grow up as a kid and transition to a teenager, you naturally make some friends along the way. Some of those friends become close enough that you label them as your best friends while your parents drift off into the background. This wasn't my case, as the one and only best friend in my life was my mom.

It's not that I was socially awkward at school, but I always felt like an outsider because all the students around me had established their friend circles early on. It didn't help that my dad was unnecessarily strict about me leaving the house after school hours. That was his way to prevent me from "fooling around" as he'd call it.

When my dad wasn't busy getting drunk and yelling at me, I passed the time by doing schoolwork, reading books, or watching movies. There was only so much that I could do within that confined space. I always longed to go to different places and explore.

Kids from school would often boast about their trips to various attractions. I used to envy the ones who were lucky enough to go to places like the Toronto Zoo, the beach, the Royal Ontario Museum, or the insanely popular theme park called Wonderland, none of which my dad ever offered to take me to. My chance to go anywhere at all was only made possible whenever my mom was at home and free to take me. What I'm witnessing in front of me is one of those precious times.

I feel nothing but happiness surging throughout my body. Happiness from spending quality time with my mom, happiness from not being stuck with my dad, and happiness from getting this rare opportunity to experience something different for a change.

"Thank you for showing this memory to me," I say to Peri. He must be wondering why I went silent as all my deep thoughts consumed me.

"There's a reason for it. A lesson which I hope you'll learn by the end of all this," Peri replies.

I'll have to wait and see what he's talking about but until then, I relish this moment. I get up from my seat and walk over to my past self and my mom as they're enjoying their meal. I stand by them so that I can listen in on their conversation.

"You have your courses picked out and you're all set. I bought you a new binder as well. High school is going to be fun Danny, don't be scared!" my mom says.

"I'm not scared mom, I just don't know what to expect," Past Danny says.

I remember what it felt like to go from elementary school to middle school to high school. It was always the sense of unfamiliarity and unpredictability that made me feel uneasy. I had turned 14 years old here and hoped that high school would treat me fairly.

While I wasn't nervous about the workload, I was intimidated by the social hierarchy because I viewed myself as being at the bottom of the food chain. I thought that I wouldn't fit into any particular group since that's how all of middle school was like for me. No matter what I feared, my mom always encouraged me and bolstered my confidence.

"I'll always be here for you. You can come talk to me about anything, whether it's about school, how you're feeling, or anything else at all," my mom says to my past self.

I feel reassured and relieved, and I can see these same emotions reflected on my past self's uplifted expression.

"Thanks mom, you're the best," Past Danny says with a smile.

"I know," my mom says with a smirk. "Now, let's finish up eating. We have our movie to catch at 6:30!"

I watch my mom give my past self the last of her fries with a smile on her face. They finish their drinks before getting up and then toss their waste into the garbage. They proceed to walk toward a door, which appears to be an exit out of the arcade. Peri also gets up from the table we were sitting at and he walks over to me.

"Looks like they're about to head out. We should do the same," Peri says.

"Can't we stay for a moment longer?" I ask. I continue to look at my past self and mom laughing and walking together.

I don't want to leave this wonderful moment behind. I've become hypnotized by the euphoria and it has a hold over me.

"We must move on Danny. It's easy to get caught up in the moment, but it's for the best," Peri says.

I don't know when I'll be able to see my mom again, but he's right. I forget that I'm in a place that technically doesn't exist, no matter how real it looks, sounds, or feels. I'm thankful for this enlightening experience, but I snap out of my delighted trance to shift my focus back on the task at hand.

"How do we leave? We got here using the door from the forest. Maybe you can do your snapping magic trick again to get us out of it?"

Peri chuckles and says, "No, unfortunately not. That snap that I did earlier was only to change the environment *within* the door. I can't use it to *leave* the door."

"So, then what? Are we stuck here?" I ask.

I stare at my past self and my mom in the distance as they're about to exit the arcade using the door in front of them. I watch my mom turn the handle but before she opens it, she pauses and turns back. She smiles for a moment, as if she sees me, and then proceeds to exit the arcade with my past self.

A mysterious shining light emerges from behind the door. It's so bright that I can't see anything past it. My past self and my mom walk right into it as if nothing is there and it doesn't seem to affect them. As the door closes behind them, I can still see the bright light shining through the small space from beneath the door.

"Could that be our way out?" I say while pointing at the exit door.

"It appears to be so," Peri replies.

We start walking toward the door that may be our ticket out of this environment. Once we arrive in front of it, I stop and look at Peri beside me.

"What happens next?" I ask.

"Your journey will continue, door by door," Peri replies.

I turn my head to face the door and I turn the handle, swinging it wide open. We're greeted by a thick bright light that shines right at us. I take a deep breath before proceeding to take some steps forward, right into the light's embrace. Peri follows suit and closes the door behind him.

The light is too bright for me to keep my eyes open so I close them shut. I feel a warm sensation that relaxes my nerves and makes me feel comfortable beyond measure. This is another opposite sensation from earlier. The door in the forest that we used to enter the memory contained nothing but ice-cold darkness. This brightly lit door that we're using to exit the memory now is much more rejuvenating and calming.

After a few moments of this pleasant experience, I feel myself going from standing up to laying down on the ground as my mind and body shift sideways on their own. The bright light behind my eyelids becomes dimmer until it's completely vanished.

As I open my eyes, the first thing that I see are leaves on the ground. I then notice Peri standing right next to me and he extends his hand to help me back up on my feet. I grasp his hand and once I'm up, I look around at where we're standing. I don't know if I've gone totally crazy yet, but we've made it back to the clearing in the dark forest. This isn't a dream after all.

THE TEST

The forest has an ominous feel to it while the moon shines above me in the night sky. There's a swarm of endless trees surrounding me, but this circular clearing acts as my haven. However, something catches my eye that doesn't fit in with the rest of the scenery. Far off in the distance, I think I see fog and what appears to be birds hovering above the trees it's covering.

I quickly realize that the fog and birds are what I noticed back when we were walking over here from the shore, when Peri told me not wander off in that direction. Is he hiding something there or is it something dangerous? Either way, it doesn't seem to be an immediate concern so I don't worry about it.

I turn my attention to where I walked through the first door. It no longer stands where it once stood as it's disappeared. What's left are the six remaining doors.

"It's gone," I say. "The first door is gone. What does that mean?"

"It means we're making progress. Slowly, but surely," Peri says. "We should continue with the remaining doors. We can't linger here for too long."

"What is this place? Is this forest real or is it something else?" I ask.

"It's complicated to explain, but you'll get your answers soon enough once we move on," Peri says. "As you complete more doors, it'll start to make more sense."

I'm wrapping my head around what we encountered in the first door while trying to guess what to expect from the remaining doors.

"Hold on, let me get the hang of this before we move. We started with seven doors and now there's six. Each of these doors contain some sort of past memory from my life. Once I walk in and experience them, I regain those pieces of my memory. Then some sort of portal opens up to bring us back here?"

"That's right, you've got the basics of it," Peri says.

I try to utilize my brain power to remember my past as much as I can. I know that the living room memory was me at around 12 years of age, and the last memory in the arcade with my mom was when I turned 14. Beyond that, my mind is totally blank and it's frustrating me.

I pull out my dead cellphone from my pocket to view my reflection staring back at me from the glass screen. I don't look anything close to 14. How much more of my memory am I really missing?

"What's my age?" I ask Peri. He hesitates to provide an answer. "I don't even remember how old I am. You can at least tell me this much information, can't you? I need to know how much of my memory I'm really missing."

Peri hesitates again before deciding to tell me. "You're 32 years old."

"What?" I ask. I start to panic as this number hits me and I realize the true peril I'm in.

I view my reflection within my phone screen again. What's going on? If I can only remember my life up until 14 right now, that means I still have a long road ahead of me. I'm missing 18 years' worth of my memories, thoughts, experiences, ideas, and opinions that I've ever accumulated. In other words, 18 years of my life that I currently have no recollection of.

Peri notices my frantic body language and distress on my face.

"It's alright, don't worry Danny. There are still six doors in front of you. Entering one door at a time is the only way to restore your memory up to where you are right now."

Who knows what lays beyond those bizarre pieces of wood? Whatever it is, I need to follow through with this and get it done as soon as possible. I need to know how I ended up here in the first place and how my mom is doing. The only way to do this is to concentrate my focus on completing each door, otherwise I don't know if I can handle all this uncertainty.

"Okay, let's go. I'm not asking any more questions for now. The sooner we get this over with, the better," I say.

"After you," Peri says. He uses his arm to direct me to the second door that's now slightly glowing, indicating that it's next in line.

Peri acts like a tour guide but there's something more to him than meets the eye. I know that there's something he's not telling me, but I'll have to be patient and wait for my answers.

We walk over to the second door that's standing in the horizontal line with the other five doors. Despite the subtle glow around it, it's an ordinary, brown-coloured wooden door with a brass doorknob. I'd expect it to be made of gold or diamonds after all the confusion I've experienced, yet it's perhaps the most "normal" looking object I've come across so far.

"These memories may be unpleasant for you, but don't forget to keep your head up." Peri says. "Remember that there are always better times ahead, and I'm going to help you see them."

I stand face-to-face with this new door, as I previously did with the first door. As long as I get more of my memory back at the end of this, I don't care what happens behind it.

"Let's see what's waiting for us on the other side then," I say.

I slowly turn the knob of the second door and anticipate what I'm about to witness. The door opens and there's nothing but pitch-black darkness inside. I take a deep breath and step forward. Peri follows me and closes the door behind us.

The darkness consumes my body and sends uncomfortable shivers down my spine. The glimmer comes to the rescue and begins forming a brand-new environment with its infinite tiny flecks. It provides enough light for me to be able to guess what's being constructed.

I begin to make out a room that contains a chalkboard, desks, chairs, textbooks, pencils, erasers, and sheets of paper, all being replicated in the highest detail. I may not have my entire memory, but I remember enough to recall what a typical classroom looks like. There are also multiple students being formed, who are sitting in their chairs behind their wooden desks. As soon as all the objects have been made by the glimmering flecks, they change their colour and at once, the vista is lit up before my eyes.

Peri and I are standing at the back of the classroom with about twenty students sitting down and facing the front. I can only see the backs of their heads as they're all viewing the chalkboard and scribbling down notes on their papers. A female teacher concludes her lesson and writes out instructions for homework underneath it.

Chapter 5, questions 25 to 38 due tomorrow. Show your work.

Some students groan and some kiss their teeth to express their frustration, but that's as far as their rebellion goes. Judging from their reactions, this must be a high school class.

"There you have it class, we'll take these questions up tomorrow. You have the rest of the class to work on them if you want less homework!"

A few students pull out their math textbook from their backpack to get a head start on the questions while others lounge back in their chair, not showing any interest whatsoever.

I must be sitting down here somewhere. Where else would I possibly be? I begin to walk around the edge of the classroom from the right side. One by one, I notice the lack of energy on the students' faces.

"As you're working on the homework questions, I'm going to hand back your unit tests. Most of you did well, but there's always room for improvement. Some of these test questions *will* show up on the final exam," says the teacher with a stack of papers in her hand. She begins to criss-cross around the classroom, returning one test at a time.

I continue to walk around the classroom in hopes of finding my past self here.

After sifting through some more desks, I come across one on the left side that's situated beside a window. There's a boy who's wearing a grey hooded sweatshirt and he's sitting up straight but not doing any work. He's simply staring out of the window, watching a gym class play a game of basketball on the court.

The teacher approaches him with a few remaining tests in her hand. She places this boy's test on his desk and draws his attention away from the basketball game.

"Danny, you need to prepare more for the next one. I'm not sure what happened, but keep practising with the homework questions," the teacher says before walking away.

The first thing he notices when he looks down at his unit test is the bright red handwriting all over the white pages. In the top right corner on the front page, a big and bold grade of *23/50,* along with the words *study harder* are written.

As this unfolds within a few seconds, my former memories and concurrent emotions of my past self hit my mind all at once.

I stumble and take a seat in an empty chair right in front of Past Danny. I feel goosebumps as I observe this out-of-body experience once more. Not only am I looking directly at my younger self, but I'm feeling the same emotions he's feeling.

So, this "trigger" that enables the return of my memories can really be *any* event. From my dad's yelling to me sinking a buzzer beater in an arcade, to now receiving an abysmal grade and feedback on a unit test. I'm starting to get the hang of this but what I'm not getting used to is experiencing these severely negative emotions infiltrating my mind from my past self. It's as if my brain is soaking up the worst feelings I had at this particular moment like a sponge.

I begin to remember where I am by recognizing my teacher, Mrs. Johnson. This is one of my old classrooms from high school and I'm sitting in my Grade 11 functions class, which was a math class I struggled in and despised. I'm 16 years old here and I can remember everything up until this point.

My eyes wander around the classroom. I notice the clock hands at 2:20 p.m., which means it's almost time for the bell to ring and everyone to go home. Instead of being excited about that, I'm feeling torment over the grade and feedback that I received on my unit test. Despite my teacher telling me to study harder, I remember that I *did* study all day and night before. This wasn't the result I was expecting because I remember aiming for a seventy percent at the very least.

I can't help but wonder why I'm feeling so upset over a measly unit test right now. It shouldn't feel like the end of the world because life is going to move forward regardless. At the delicate age of 16 though, these kinds of obstacles can be insurmountable. I begin to remember the reasoning behind this specific feeling of devastation and defeat.

As I was growing up, I would often hear stories and anecdotes from my parents that would usually involve their upbringing in the country of India throughout the 1960s and 70s.

Their parents before them were simple farmers from a small village, and so were their parents before them. My parents told me that the only education they completed was up to high school and they never had the opportunity to attend any college or university. They immigrated to the city of Brampton in the early

1980s while they were in their 20s. They were young but their decision to leave their home country and start a new life halfway around the world meant that it would hopefully provide a better future for their child.

As I became more knowledgeable about their circumstances, I started to realize how much my parents sacrificed for me to be here. I started to feel more weight on my shoulders as the years passed by. I always tried my best in school to make them as proud as possible, but what started out as motivation soon turned into a downward slope.

I began viewing myself more as a justification for their decision to immigrate here instead of viewing myself as my own person. Whenever I received a "C" on an essay, a 23/50 on a math test, or any other anomaly of a grade that stood out, it absolutely shattered my confidence, ambition, and self-esteem.

Grades 9 and 10 flew by with relative ease but as soon as I made it to Grade 11, my mindset changed and it slowly began to take a toll on me.

I knew that I had to get more serious about my education than I already was if I ever wanted to be admitted to a college or university. My parents were never able to attend, so it was up to me to change the course of our family history. My math grades were on a steady decline and as the months went on, my overall average began to suffer. There were many days when I felt down and hopeless because I thought I wasn't going to be accepted anywhere after high school.

My parents never wanted me to obsess over post-secondary education like this, but I felt like it was something that I desperately needed to achieve or else they'd view me differently.

I used to have this image in my head that depicted the upper years of high school as being the most exciting and adventurous, making you feel like you're on top of the world. A few weeks into Grade 11 and I realized that image was far from reality.

It wasn't as fun as I had envisioned, as I constantly beat myself up over lower grades and not being able to maintain any sort of balance. Instead of joining a club or a sports team like I usually did in previous years, I couldn't stop thinking about what I was going to do and where I was going to go after high school.

It seemed as if everyone else was on track to succeed and had a clear plan for their future except me. I constantly worried about this added pressure and I feared my classmates laughing at me or ridiculing me.

Peri breaks up my troublesome thoughts and taps me on the shoulder.

"How are you holding up?" he asks.

"I don't know, not too well. More of my memories came back to me but I feel down and beaten again. I feel whatever my past self is feeling," I say as I nod my head in the direction of my mirror image in front of me.

Past Danny isn't viewing the unit test or working on any homework questions but instead, watching the gym class play basketball outside of the window again.

Peri sits on top of a desk beside me and faces my direction. Mrs. Johnson and the other students continue to move and work in the background behind him.

"You *thought* you were beaten here. It's all about perspective. At this moment in your life, the only thing that mattered to you was receiving good grades. Whenever you didn't, you thought you were a failure instead of thinking about how you tried your best," Peri says.

"All I ever wanted was to make my parents proud of me. I didn't want them to think that their one and only son was a disappointment," I say.

"What was the real cost of you trying to make them proud? The constant stress? The all-nighters? Your own happiness?" Peri asks.

"I thought that sacrifices needed to be made if you wanted to achieve your goals. Just like my parents sacrificed leaving their home country to come here," I say.

"Instead of using that as a bit of motivation, you took it as a burden upon yourself," Peri says. "I'm sure you remember how good you were in other things. History class for one. Or what about exercising and all the sports teams you used to play on? Basketball, soccer, volleyball."

"What does any of that stuff matter if I couldn't even pass a stupid math test like this one?" I say while looking down at the unit test on my past self's desk. "I don't even remember what grade I ended up with in this class because that part of my memory is still blocked off. Did I earn the credit for this class and did I graduate?"

"You'll recall those details the further we progress, but try to control these emotions for now Danny," Peri says. He then gets up from the desk he's sitting on and looks at me as if he's struck up some new idea. "I have something that'll help you understand and feel better. Shall we leave and move on?" Peri asks.

"Move on where?" I ask.

"A more hopeful time," Peri says.

"Why are you showing this memory to me anyway? What's all of this supposed to mean in the end?" I ask.

"If I tell you now, it'll defeat the entire purpose. Keep in mind that I'm trying to help you and I'm on your side. You're doing good so far," Peri says.

"Alright, if you say so… Let's go then, it's not like I have much of a choice," I say.

"Onward to a better time," Peri says.

Peri holds his fingers out in front of him. As soon as he snaps them, everything around us fades away. The classroom, the desks, Mrs. Johnson, my former classmates, and my disappointing unit test all disappear into nothingness until we're standing in complete darkness again. A new environment begins to take form as the glimmer goes to work while I wait in silence.

Once the new environment has been completed, Peri and I are standing at the back of what appears to be another room, which is smaller than my living room and the classroom. A lamp shines in the corner, sitting atop a long rectangular desk and providing the only source of light. There are two people sitting across from each other at opposite sides of the desk.

I instantly recognize my past self sitting on one end because his face hasn't drastically changed from a few moments ago. I remember that I often wore plaid shirts in high school, and this blue full-sleeved shirt was one of my favourites. This new memory can't be too far ahead from my math class.

Sitting across the desk from my past self is another man who seems to be older. He doesn't appear to be a teacher though, especially since this doesn't resemble anything close to a classroom. It's more of a formal setting, closer to looking like an office.

The man is wearing unusually framed reading glasses and he has a stern look on his face. However, as soon as he starts speaking, his voice is gentle and friendly.

"I'm going to be honest with you Danny. Everyone's bound to have failures and doubts in their lives. I've had plenty of them myself. But remember this, it's how you react to them that defines you as a person," the man tells Past Danny, sitting with his hands together in his lap.

"It feels like I'm about to lose a race because I don't know what I want to do after high school," Past Danny says as the man carefully observes him.

"Do you think I always knew that I would end up becoming a guidance counsellor here and helping students like you when I was only in high school? No Danny. Everyone has ups and downs, and everyone needs time to figure out what they really want to do with their lives. It takes longer for some people than others, and that's completely fine," explains the man.

As soon as the man says these words of reassurance to my past self, I feel more memories coming back to my mind. I don't stagger, but I put a hand to my temple to relax.

This memory we're in right now is taking place a few months after the last memory in the math classroom. It's not a drastic jump in the time gap, so that may explain why I'm better able to cope with it. I feel the same emotions as my past self sitting in his chair and I remember everything up until the end of the eleventh grade.

Peri looks over at me and realizes that the trigger has worked to restore part of my memory. A few minutes ago, I failed to see any kind of relevance with what was happening in front of me. Now that I have more of my memories flooded back into my mind, the context of this environment has changed entirely.

I remember that the man sitting on the other side of the desk was my guidance counsellor, Mr. Baker. Out of all the teachers I had in high school, he was the one person I could openly talk to about anything. Whether it was about my life at home or my academic problems, he never judged me and always understood what I was going through.

I felt that I couldn't talk about my lower school grades with my parents because I had this picture in my head where they'd view me as incompetent. I had very few friends at the time, and they were also out of the question because doing well in school was never their priority. I couldn't talk to my teachers about my performance either because they weren't encouraging enough and would unknowingly put me down more than I already was.

Scribbling comments like *study harder* on a unit test only made me want to study *less* because I started to give up. Mr. Baker single-handedly saved me from that negative mentality, as he was there for me in a way that no one else was throughout my high school years. This little guidance office became my haven from the rest of the school.

Mr. Baker scrolls through a program on his computer next to him before addressing Past Danny again.

"I see here that you didn't end up with the best of grades in your math class, but you can retake it in summer school and improve it. Also, have you considered staying back for an extra semester to improve your average? That's always an option too. Every student feels this rush and urge to leave high school right away, but slow and steady wins the race," Mr. Baker says.

I can see Past Danny sigh and drop his head down. I feel his lingering frustration, but there's also a part of him that's starting to see a bit of reason.

"That's easy to say, but my situation is totally different. I don't have that sort of time on my hands. I need to graduate on time and then get into a college the same year," Past Danny says.

"I know you feel a certain type of pressure to appease your parents from what you've told me before, but slow down for a second. It seems like ever since this school year started, you've become a different person. You're much more serious and anxious now. You weren't like this last year," Mr. Baker says.

My past self looks at Mr. Baker as he continues to put the "guide" in guidance.

"When was the last time you took a small break to relax?" Mr. Baker asks.

"It's been a while with all that's going on recently," Past Danny responds.

"Maybe you can start going to the gym again? I haven't seen you in there for weeks now.

"I don't know, maybe," Past Danny says.

"Believe me when I tell you that your parents are already proud of you, and so am I. You're an amazing student and a role model in this school. Please, try not to burn yourself out Danny. I've seen what that does to students. It'll take a toll on you," Mr. Baker says.

I feel my past self experiencing more optimism now.

"I'll try. Do you think I'll be able to get into a good college?" Past Danny asks.

"I don't think so. I *know* so. You have loads of potential within you, so work on letting go of your fears and self-doubt," Mr. Baker says.

Past Danny expresses a small smile as Mr. Baker continues his motivational talk.

"Education is great to have, but it isn't everything. Your history mark was pretty high, so you should know better than anyone that some of the most influential people never went to any college or university. It's not the only path in the world. Anyway, you're only 16 years old. You have a whole life ahead of you. What matters most is trying your best in whatever you do. You're going to do great and become somebody, I know it," Mr. Baker says while looking at Past Danny with a smile.

"Thank you for that. I didn't know I needed to hear all this but I'm glad I came down today. How are you able to speak like that and motivate people so easily?" Past Danny asks with a chuckle.

"Believe it or not, I was a very shy student back when I was in high school. I never used to raise my hand whenever my teachers would ask a question because I feared what other students would think about me. Eventually, there came a time when I decided to face that fear head on, so I began working on my communication skills as I grew older. You can do anything you want, as long as you learn something from the valuable lessons that life has in store for us. There's a saying that I heard once when I was in your shoes, from one of my own teachers. *Never stop learning because life never stops teaching*," Mr. Baker says.

"I'll work on improving myself like you did, and I'll try to remember that one," Past Danny says.

Mr. Baker stands up from his chair and appears to have one final thought in his head. "Actually, let me change it up for you. *Life is a test and failure is your best teacher*," Mr. Baker says. He then pats my past self's shoulder as he walks toward his office door. "Keep that one in mind Danny. Now, I have a meeting with another student at 11:30 in the next building, but I'm always here to talk when you need to."

With that said, my past self also stands up and faces Mr. Baker with a grin.

"Thank you so much for everything, honestly," Past Danny says. He shakes Mr. Baker's hand and I experience a tremendous warm feeling on the inside from this whole interaction.

"I'll check in with you some time again in the next few weeks," Past Danny says as he puts his backpack on. "I'll see you in the gym as well."

"Sounds great Danny. Drop in any time you're free or make an appointment if I'm not in my office," Mr. Baker says as he opens the door. Past Danny walks out and Mr. Baker follows.

The door closes behind Mr. Baker, as Peri and I are left in his office to think about what just happened. After a few moments, Peri finally breaks the silence.

"Something as small as that conversation can have a huge impact on someone's life. You were lucky to have someone like that as your guidance counsellor. He turned your worries into opportunities for learning and he always reassured you that you weren't alone," Peri says.

"He's one of the few who really cared. He was never fake and he genuinely wanted to help me. You can say that about very few teachers in your life," I say.

I wish that weren't true but it's the reality within most school systems. Not every teacher is bad but not every teacher is good. More often than not, many of the good teachers eventually turn bad as their motivation decreases over the years. That initial spark of determination and curiosity naturally fades away, and what's left is a bunch of educators who fail to see that their lack of enthusiasm easily rubs off on their own students.

Since elementary school, I remember about three or four teachers who stood out to me and put in effort to make their classrooms an exciting hub for learning. Getting an awesome teacher for one of your classes was like winning the lottery, based entirely on luck and timing. The rest of the teachers always seemed miserable so in turn, their students became miserable.

We don't get to choose who our teachers are going to be, so the trajectory of our academic careers can drastically change with who we end up with. We can either get the best of role models or the most mediocre and bad apples of the bunch. Because I had more from the latter, I'm glad that I was at least able to have an incredible guidance counsellor who did exactly what his position entailed. Mr. Baker guided my decision-making throughout high school, and he provided informative counsel whenever I needed it. Most of all, he listened to me and whatever I had to say, which made me comfortable in expressing my deepest thoughts to him.

It's extremely easy to *hear* someone when they speak and totally forget about what they're saying the next second because their problems aren't your own. On the other hand, it's much more challenging to truly *listen* to someone, comprehend their situation, and empathize with them when they need your support. Mr. Baker listened to me, and I'll always be thankful for his assistance throughout one of the most stressful times in my life.

"How do you feel now?" Peri asks as he interrupts my thoughts.

"Much better than how I was feeling in the classroom after I got that unit test slapped on my desk. These 'better' memories that you're showing me after you snap your fingers are like small antidotes of relief. I felt this same response in the arcade with my mom. They make me feel a sense of happiness and confidence," I say.

"I'm glad you feel that way," Peri says. "Again, you may think that there's been a lot of negative times in your life, but there's just as many positive times if you dig deep within yourself to find them. They may not be as big or as memorable, but they're there."

If Peri continues to show me memories like these ones from high school, then I'm pretty sure I'll be able to handle them. However, my gut feeling tells me that there'll be much tougher ones ahead as I grow older. Either way, I'm glad I was able to see Mr. Baker again and listen to his encouraging words one more time, even if it was within a supernatural setting.

"Thanks for showing me this moment. I didn't realize how articulate Mr. Baker was whenever he spoke. I'll remember his words of wisdom, as I'll remember yours," I say.

"That's all it is Danny, one life lesson to the next. One door to the next. Are you ready to move on?" Peri asks.

"I'm ready," I say.

I need to move on in hopes of recovering more of my memories. I take a final look at this guidance office that I used to visit as a young and naive student. Who knows if I'll ever see it again?

I notice a shining bright light appear underneath the office door that Past Danny and Mr. Baker exited from, similar to the exit door at the arcade.

"There's that same light," I say.

"Yes, there's our cue to leave the memory. After you," Peri says with his arms directed toward the door.

I open Mr. Baker's office door and there's nothing but a bright, shining white light. It appears to be the exact same light from the arcade when it was time for us to leave.

As I step inside the door, the blinding light completely engulfs me. Mr. Baker's office disappears as Peri closes the door behind him.

I decide to close my eyes and I patiently await what happens next. Just like before, being in this exit door feels much more comfortable, soothing, and warm compared to the piercing, cold, dark door I used to enter. The journey toward regaining my memory and my identity continues.

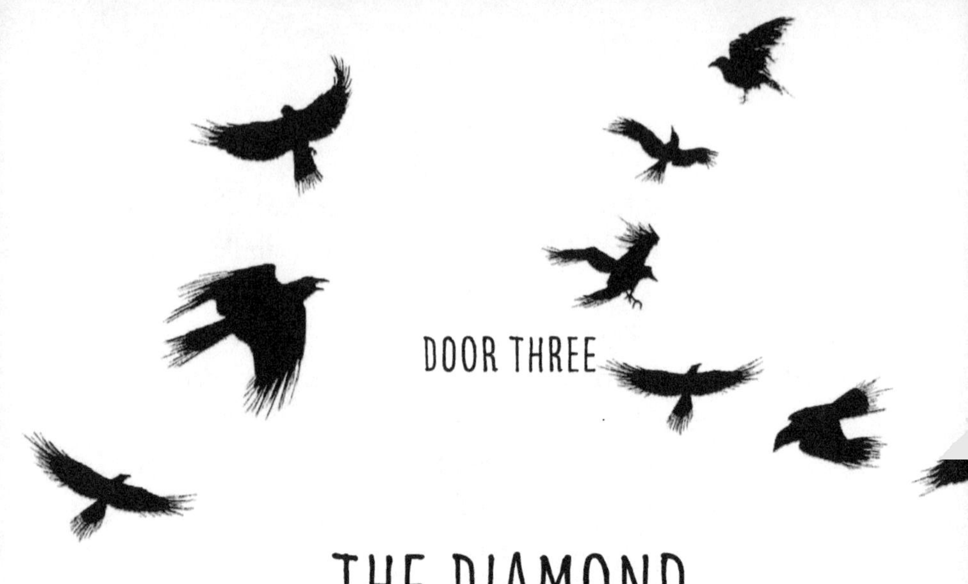

DOOR THREE

THE DIAMOND

As I regain my vison, I let out a sigh as I'm back in the dreaded forest that I'm anxiously trying to escape. On the plus side, I remember everything from my life until the age of 16 now. It's not much considering that's only half my present age and there's many more years to reclaim, but it's a start.

The second door has vanished behind me so that can be marked off my to-do list. Two down, five to go. I know this challenge is going to take a while at this rate, so I try to speed things along as quickly as I can.

I look around for Peri to tell him that I'm ready to move on and enter the next door, but he's not here for some reason. I walk around the clearing and check behind the doors for any signs of him but there's nothing here. The forest outside this space contains a dark atmosphere and my mind tells me not venture into it. This little clearing within this vast forest makes me feel safe, even though I don't want to stay here a second longer than I need to.

"Peri!" I shout as I search behind the doors again. I don't receive any response. I walk to the very edge of the clearing, right up to where the trees border around it.

"PERI!" I shout louder.

No response again. I try looking into the dense forest to see if he's out there somewhere. I notice the same thick fog that I saw before, along with the same birds hovering above it. The fog is gradually devouring the trees in its path as it crawls forward, and those aren't any regular birds. They appear to be black crows and I can hear their gurgling croaks, which deeply unsettle me. They're still a great distance away but they're moving closer to me, which I'm assuming isn't a good sign.

Behind me, from the opposite end of the circular clearing, I hear a familiar voice.

"Danny, I'm over here," Peri says as he emerges from the forest behind him.

"What were you doing in there?" I ask.

"I was speaking with the one who sent me to you. He told me that we're moving too slowly. We need to hurry along or else you'll risk failing this trial," Peri says.

He speaks casually for someone bringing up more confusing information to the forefront.

"What trial? Speaking with who?" I ask.

"The one who sent me here, my master. I didn't show up at the shore by chance," Peri says.

"What master? Is he someone like you? Is this whole thing his game or something? Why doesn't he reveal himself instead of using you as a messenger?" I ask. I'm bombarding Peri with questions to hopefully get an answer. I'm sure that they won't make any sense to me regardless, but it's worth a shot.

"It's the entity I serve. He's putting you through this trial for a reason and it's better not to question his motives," Peri says. "He can't take on a physical form, so I represent his interests."

"I have no idea what you guys want from me because I have nothing to give you. I don't know why I'm being tested in this 'trial.' I just want to leave and go back to where I came from, that's all," I say.

"It's not that we want something from you. I already know what's behind these doors. It's more about getting you to see what they contain and learn something from them. That can only happen if we focus on the task at hand. Now let us make use of our time and move forward," Peri says.

"This still doesn't make much sense to me. And I was trying to move on, but you weren't here," I say.

"Apologies Danny, you're right. I won't disappear on you like that again." He looks out toward the forest and notices the same fog and crows in the distance that I was viewing earlier. "We're losing enough time as it is," he says.

I was right, there's something about that fog after all. I save my remaining questions and thoughts for later as we walk toward the third door.

This plain door will be responsible for giving me back some of my memory, but not without subjugating me to some mental trauma first.

My alcoholic dad and poor academic performance may have only been two small cogs in the overall wheel of my damaged mind. Issues can become more hurtful and impactful the older you grow, so this roller coaster may not be slowing down any time soon. I'm hoping that whatever I experience next doesn't make me feel any worse but knowing my luck so far, it probably will.

I turn the knob of the third door with a glow around it. I slowly push the knob forward and as the door opens, I view the extensive empty blackness within it.

I step inside and close my eyes, patiently waiting to find out about what I must endure next. I feel cold and I wish that I could regain my memory without experiencing or remembering any of the bad times in my life.

I can feel the glimmer moving around me as the ghostly environment begins to take shape. After a few moments, I open my eyes to see that the magic is done and the new environment has been constructed.

This new environment is much larger in scope compared to the living room, arcade, classroom, and guidance office from the previous memories.

We seem to be standing in an open field beside a recreation centre on a nice summer day. There's a deserted baseball diamond right in front of it. All around this space, the flowers have bloomed, the grass is green, the sky is blue, and everything seems to be perfect. There's no one around us besides a group of people sitting on the bleachers behind the baseball diamond. I'm guessing my past self must be one of those individuals as there are no other options to consider.

I start walking toward the group, wondering what's about to happen but more importantly, what I'm about to feel. I pass by a large sign that displays *Sportsplex*, which must be the name of this place.

As Peri and I move closer to the group, I begin to sense that something is off. I can overhear a girl talking, along with two boys who don't sound anything like me. Once we arrive and stand next to this trio, I confirm that my past self isn't present among them.

"I'm not even here, what is this?" I ask Peri. "Who are these people?"

"Patience," Peri responds. His one word is enough to keep me silent for now and focus on observing the individuals in front of me.

"Take a swig of this," a lanky boy says as he offers a flask to the other two. They take a few sips and exhale loudly. I'm pretty sure they're not drinking chocolate milk, as I recall my dad displaying the same expression countless times.

"Good stuff, for real," the girl with red hair says.

"Smoother than the crap you brought last week," says the other boy, who's much bulkier in size than everyone else here.

"Come on, I told you that was some stuff that I took from my dad's cupboard. I didn't know it'd end up being moonshine," the lanky boy says.

"If it's sitting in a jar that doesn't look like a bottle, it's obviously moonshine you idiot," retorts the bigger boy.

"Whatever man. If I ever start my own distillery, you're not invited!" the lanky boy says with a chuckle.

This conversation reminds me of my dad. He would drink anything if it had even one percent of alcohol in it. I turn around and view the landscape around us. There's a road that's not too far away with no traffic running on it, along with a sidewalk with no pedestrians.

"So, what were you guys up to last night?" the girl asks.

"Same old. Got high and played video games," the lanky boy says.

"Went to the gym… *then* got high and played video games," the bigger boy says before they all start snickering together.

"Hold on, look at what we have here," the girl says while looking right at me. I panic for a second, thinking she's noticed me and Peri.

My panic subsides as she stands up from her seat and starts looking past me at the sidewalk. I turn around and notice someone riding a bicycle across our view.

"Danny! Over here!" the girl yells to the cyclist.

The figure on the sidewalk, presumably my past self, briefly notices the girl's calls but keeps his head straight. He doesn't bother responding and continues to ride forward. It seems as if he's purposely avoiding this group and pretending that he didn't hear her.

"The nerve of this guy," the lanky boy says.

The bigger boy gets up from his seat to join the girl and forms a megaphone with his hands over his mouth. He then proceeds to yell as loud as he can.

"HEY DANNY, COME OVER HERE!"

His words are loud enough to successfully draw my past self's attention. He diverges from his path and begins to ride his bike toward the baseball diamond.

"Oh, great," I say to Peri. "I'm sure this interaction will be a smooth one…"

I begin to recognize my past self's face as he steadily travels across the green grass and approaches us. I look older and more tired than the last time I saw myself in Mr. Baker's office.

Past Danny arrives on the scene and hits the breaks on his bike a few metres away from the bleachers. He's wearing blue running shoes with silver shorts and a white t-shirt.

"Hey guys, what's up?" Past Danny asks the trio. He gets off his bike, kicks the stand in place, and approaches the group. He bumps each person's fist with his own as they stare at him unenthusiastically.

"Harold… Sophie… Mike. What's new? How've you guys been?"

"We're good, what's up with you? You've been ducking our messages and calls, eh?" asks Harold, the lanky boy.

"I haven't been ducking anything. I've been busy lately," Past Danny replies.

"Busy with what?" asks Mike, the bigger boy.

"I've been working in my mom's factory with her over the summer. By the time I get home, I'm drained," Past Danny says.

"Cool story, but aren't you free on weekends? We haven't properly hung out in months," Harold pushes on.

"I also have this summer school course I'm working on," Past Danny explains. "I've been using the free time I have on weekends to keep up with that."

I can hear the subtle nervousness in my past self's voice. This conversation has abruptly shifted into an interrogation and it's obvious that he doesn't want to be here.

"Interesting. What are you doing out here then? Don't you have some homework to do?" Mike asks.

"Leave him alone guys," Sophie says while inspecting Past Danny from top to bottom with her piercing eyes. "He's not worth it, never was."

"I thought I'd get some fresh air for once, so I'm out for a quick bike ride around the block," Past Danny says, ignoring Sophie's comment.

"You're saying that you could've hung out with us today, but you chose to go out for your little bike ride instead?" Mike asks.

I see the frustration building up on my past self's face and his body language changes after that last verbal jab.

"Seriously, what's with all the questions man? I don't have to justify anything to you," Past Danny snaps.

Mike doesn't take kindly to that reaction, so he jumps down from the bleachers and walks right up to Past Danny. With both of his hands, Mike shoves Past Danny back with enough force to cause him to trip and fall to the ground.

It's at this very moment that more of my former memories come racing back to my mind, causing me to stagger next to Peri. He helps me sit down on the bleachers as my mind attempts to contain everything it's become exposed to.

"Better talk to us with some respect Danny boy. Don't forget, you used to call us brothers in high school. Now look at how you switched up on us. You think you're too good for us college boy?" Mike asks.

College boy? So, I did graduate high school and made it to post-secondary after all.

More memories come back to my mind by the second. This specific one occurring in front of me is taking place during the summer break, some time in July, after I completed my first year of college. That places me at around 18 years of age here.

There's not much time to reminisce about the past as there's still chaos unfolding in front of me. I'm feeling exactly what my past self is experiencing as he lays defenceless on the ground: a lot of anger, anxiety, and fear of what's to come next as Mike stands above him like a giant.

Peri and I are sitting by the sidelines and watching the emotions exponentially flare up within everyone.

My past self picks himself up off the ground and looks at Mike right in his eyes. Past Danny balls a fist up with his right hand, but he decides to show restraint instead.

"It's not like that Mike, believe me. I needed some time alone this summer and I've been in my own zone lately. It's nothing personal at all," Past Danny says.

"You can't even hang out with us once a month or something? That sounds pretty whack to me," Harold says, disregarding any logic that my past self is attempting to explain.

Arguments among friends can be some of the worst you can ever have in your life. A small molehill of a disagreement can become a divisive mountain of animosity. Friendships can be made or broken within minutes. I'm unfortunately witnessing the latter.

I feel the anger surging throughout my past self. It's as if Past Danny's on trial with a jury that's determined to proclaim a guilty verdict. They're not listening to a single thing he has to say, so he decides to break his self-control and voice his honest opinions out loud.

"No that's not whack, *you're* whack. Listen, I came here out of good will but you guys are showing none to me. No disrespect, but all you guys do is get drunk and high. There's a time and place for everything. I used to be cool with it on occasion but it's all you ever do now. When are you going to change things up and start taking life more seriously?" Past Danny asks.

"Excuse me, but who are you to say something like that?" Sophie asks.

"That's it, I've had enough of this clown," Mike says. He stomps toward my past self and viciously swings his balled-up fist. He narrowly misses as Past Danny dodges it by quickly ducking down.

"What are you doing? You've lost it man," Past Danny says while backing away and creating some space in between them.

Mike is relentless though. He was on the football team in high school and was known for his ruthless tackles. Mike charges directly at Past Danny and makes contact with his left shoulder.

I feel my past self's urgency to protect himself, mixed in with loads of anger toward the entire trio. Past Danny swings back at Mike and lands a punch square in his jaw. Mike rapidly recovers and continues his mission to inflict pain on Past Danny. At this point, Harold also jumps down from the bleachers and runs behind Past Danny, encircling him in a trap.

"Here, I'll help you!" yells Harold. He grabs Past Danny from behind with his skinny arms and restrains him long enough to present him as a prize to Mike's fury.

"Screw it guys, let him go!" Sophie unconvincingly shouts from her seat.

I'm clenching my teeth as I feel the same panic as Past Danny. Mike's solid fist lands a powerful punch in his stomach and knocks the wind out of him.

My past self tries to kick back out of desperation, but his attempts are useless. Mike punches him a few more times before he decides to stop his onslaught. Once enough damage has been dealt, Harold lets go of Past Danny from behind and he falls to the ground again. He's completely defeated and he doesn't get up quickly this time.

While I can't feel the physical pain that my past self is enduring in front of me, I can feel his mental pain. Nothing but regret and frustration is swirling around in my mind, as my past self is thinking about why he ever became friends with this group of people in the first place.

"This guy thought he could come over here and show us what's good," Mike says as he chuckles and walks back to the bleachers.

"Don't worry Danny, I'll get you some of my dad's moonshine to help you recover. You'll need it," Harold says and howls with laughter as he crouches down beside Past Danny.

"He doesn't drink like us remember. We're a bunch of degenerates. He's a good kid who'd rather read books," Sophie says.

Past Danny, who's down, beaten, and ridiculed, sluggishly picks himself back up with the limited amount of strength he has left. Blood is dripping from his nostrils and grass stains are visible on his white t-shirt. Past Danny turns around without saying anything to the group and limps over to his bike nearby.

He kicks the stand up, takes a seat, and slowly pushes the pedals to ride back to the sidewalk he originally diverted from.

"Have a good summer Danny!" Mike yells, attempting to rub salt in Past Danny's wounds with one last insult.

Past Danny doesn't turn around or respond, as he gets smaller in the distance with each passing second.

"This one really stings," I say to Peri. I stand up from my seat and begin to walk away from the group. I don't want to listen to a single word of their conversation anymore. "I used to think Sophie was a good friend and Mike wasn't wrong about what he said. I considered those guys to be my brothers in high school, especially since I had no siblings. But this isn't what brothers do."

"What happened was unfortunate Danny, there's no doubt about it. But try to view it as a learning experience," Peri says.

"What learning experience!?" I fiercely ask. "Learning not to trust anyone? Because that's what happened after this fight."

"That's not true," Peri says.

I ignore him and continue walking across the green field, becoming lost in my own thoughts for a moment.

I remember everything up until the end of this summer, as second year of college was approaching. This was one of those incidents in my life that affected me on a whole different level because I hadn't experienced it before. It was an incident that propelled the deterioration of my mental health and trust in other people. I remember I fell into a deep slump for the rest of that summer, completely isolating myself at home within my bedroom. It was my safe space, and I would only leave it to go to the bathroom or go downstairs to the kitchen.

It genuinely hurts when close friendships don't work out. It's said that good things must come to an end, but sometimes those good things crash and burn like a disastrous fire. The worst part about friendships being shattered is when you occasionally reminisce about all the good times you once had.

These memories become engrained within your brain, no matter how hard you try to forget about them and move on. You think about all the times you had a friend's utmost trust and loyalty, childishly believing that those unbreakable bonds would last forever. You think about where it all went wrong and what could've saved that friendship.

No matter what the reason may be for its demise, it's a distinctive kind of pain when your best friends for two years can become total strangers within two months. That's what happened between me, Mike, Harold, and Sophie.

The four of us became great friends at the start of Grade 12 and we were pretty much inseparable up until this point. I'm thinking about all the birthday parties we went to, movie nights we planned, video game sessions we enjoyed, and random inside jokes we shared. That all changed when I attended college and became busier with my studies and work. Instead of supporting me, my supposed friends turned on me because they didn't have the patience to deal with my absence whenever they hung out. Our friendship, that once seemed to be indestructible, quickly crumbled and went down the drain.

I deserve some of the blame for that happening because of my lack of communication, but I always thought about how I had bigger goals in my life that I needed to achieve by working hard. I couldn't afford to waste time like they did so after a while, I switched gears and refrained from reaching out to them as often as I used to.

They took the matter more personally than I expected and they couldn't handle it as maturely as I thought they would. This altercation that I witnessed in front of me was the result of a few months' worth of tension and build-up between us. It's one thing for a friendship to end naturally with dying communication, but it's another issue entirely when it concludes with physical violence and verbal insults being hurled in person.

Your emotional wall weakens and you start to trust people much less than before, which is exactly what happened to me once I saw that trio's true colours. Trusting someone is a peculiar concept. It can take many months, if not years, to build up but it can also come crashing down within seconds. It can be so fragile at times that you start to question if it's even worth building at all.

"Real friends are hard to come by," Peri says, breaking my chain of thought. "These weren't your real friends."

"I didn't expect them to switch up on me like this and get so aggressive with me. They got upset because I chose to spend more time on my books and work instead of alcohol and smoking," I say as we continue walking across the field.

I can hear the discomfort in my voice because I never thought I'd have to experience this incident again.

"Everything happens for a reason," Peri says. "There's always better people out there in the world, even if you think there's not."

"I know that but so far, it seems like my life automatically gravitates toward the bad ones," I say.

"Let me show you some of the good ones then," Peri says.

Peri stops in his tracks in the middle of the field and holds up his hand. He then snaps his fingers and everything around us fades to black. The blue sky, green field, colourful flowers, and my old bicycle in the distance vanish without a trace. The glimmer begins to weave a new environment in its place.

I close my eyes to try to remember what happened after this fight with my former group of friends, but no luck. I spend the next few moments taking deep breaths to try to relax my nerves. However, my mind won't easily rest because it keeps thinking about Mike shoving me to the ground, Harold assisting him, and Sophie enjoying the show.

Peri intervenes and seizes my attention once he speaks.

"You may want to open your eyes for this one."

I open my eyes and my jaw drops as low as it can once this new environment fills up with colour. The enormous scope and scale of this environment is the largest yet. Mother nature has been replaced with tall concrete buildings. The sky has been exchanged with bright neon lights. The emptiness of the field around us is now covered in roads that are littered with thousands of pedestrians. I don't know what's going on, but Peri and I are undoubtedly standing in the middle of Times Square in New York City! Well, this sure is a change of scenery.

My senses are taking in the unlimited sights and sounds around us. Bright billboards, flashy advertisements, yellow taxi cabs, talented street performers, enticing retail stores, craveable fast food restaurants, tourists taking pictures, and towering skyscrapers. I'm in awe staring at this perfect replica of one of the most famous intersections on the planet as absolutely none of it appears to be out of place.

I force myself to snap out my hypnotized trance when I realize I'm praising this fake reality a bit too much.

"This is crazy. Do you mind telling me why we're standing in Times Square? I ask Peri.

"Oh, it's nothing… Just a little vacation. Wait and see, you'll like this one," Peri says.

This place is nowhere near the size of the previous environments. How am I supposed to find my past self in these immense crowds of people around us? I start wondering about where I would be if I were actually here right now. Everywhere I look, there are so many little shops and food places that I could be in.

As my eyes are wandering, I notice something holds my gaze. There's a large area underneath the central billboard that could be a good option to explore. It contains vibrant red steps where tons of people are relaxing and taking pictures. I decide to go with my gut feeling and I begin walking in that direction with Peri following behind me.

We walk right through the crowds and we arrive at these distinctive red steps that many people are sitting on. They remind me of the bleachers behind the baseball diamond. I look around but don't see my past self anywhere. I start walking up the plentiful steps in front of me to gain a better vantage point from the very top.

Once I'm there, I view the entire vista in front of me. It's a complete mishmash of pedestrians, cars, and lights, which makes the previous environments look like a kid's playground in comparison.

"How am I supposed to find myself in all this?" I ask Peri standing next to me.

"Hmm… Try to follow your voice," Peri says.

I'm not sure if that's a solid strategy but I'll try it out anyway. I close my eyes and try to drown out as much of the noise around me as I can. New York City isn't exactly the quietest of places.

I listen extra carefully as my eyes remain closed and my body remains planted in place. I manage to isolate a few conversations on both sides of me before deciding to take a step down and listen to some more of them. People are talking and discussing all kinds of topics, from the weather to the traffic, their plans for the day, where they're staying, and what they bought while shopping.

I continue to take a step down with each conversation I fixate on and filter out. As I'm seven steps down from where I started, I listen to one particular conversation that sounds energetic and humorous.

"Okay, that street performer was awesome but creepy at the same time, if that makes sense," a girl says.

"That mime *totally* had a thing for you," a boy teases her.

"Are you kidding me? I think he wanted your number before you walked away from him," the girl jokes back.

"Welcome to NYC I guess," another boy chimes in, whose voice sounds familiar enough for me to open my eyes.

I walk over to this trio that's a few metres away as they continue with their conversation.

"I can do the same impression for free," the same boy says. He then starts acting like a mime himself and makes the other two individuals laugh.

That surely can't be me acting like that… can it?

I arrive beside the group and analyze all three of their faces one by one. The girl has curly brown hair and is wearing a jean jacket while the boy beside her has a fitted New York Yankees cap on his head and a white t-shirt. The third individual, who's providing his best performance as a mime, has short, styled hair and is wearing a brown leather jacket, along with a vintage watch and a pair of beige, suede boots. That's definitely something I would've worn, and his face resembles a younger version of mine.

"Oh come on Danny, that's not even close! You need a career change," the girl says as she's laughing.

The memories come flooding back into my mind all at once. I begin to experience an adrenaline rush of excitement, happiness, and comfort. There's my old self right in front of me with two new companions.

"Peri, over here! I found myself!" I shout behind me.

Peri walks down the steps to check in on me.

"Is everything alright? Did it work? Did you get more of your memories back?" Peri asks.

"I remember all of this," I say with a massive grin on my face. I feel like I'm on another planet with the amount of enjoyment within my mind, which is exactly what Past Danny is feeling in front of me. Joyous sensations are flowing throughout my body as if it's been given an antidote for the sadness and weakness from before. It's the total opposite of the poisonous altercation I experienced at the baseball diamond.

"This was the very *next* summer break, after my second year of college. I think it was some time in late August after my birthday, so I had recently turned 20," I say.

Past Danny looks completely overjoyed to be where he is and he's living in the moment. He's standing tall and appears to be much more confident compared to the last time I saw him when he was vulnerable.

Past Danny uses both of his hands to operate a camera that's strapped around his neck. He begins taking pictures of the square and his friends. As he does so, I use this time to recall my newly restored memories.

"Give me a moment. I need to know what happened in the past year," I say to Peri.

He silently nods his head and I begin to drift off in my thoughts. I start thinking about what led to this very moment in my life.

After that incident with Mike, Harold, and Sophie, I felt constant dread, frustration, and hopelessness. It didn't help that it took place right before my second year of college started because I needed support.

Graduating from high school is like pushing the reset button on your social life. People you may have regularly interacted with in your local area since elementary school may never be seen or heard from again. As you attend a college or university, there's an opportunity to meet new people who are attending from different parts of the world. You have a chance to start building connections and a sense of independence for yourself, but I initially struggled with that.

I was alone in college from day one, as I was the only student from my high school to enroll there. Throughout my first year, I usually went straight to my lectures and then straight home. I didn't want to live on residence, and I didn't linger on campus any longer than I needed to.

The fight in the summer break after my first year made matters much worse because I lost the three friends that I considered close to me. That confrontation had a bigger toll on me than I expected, and I didn't know how to cope with my situation. I felt that I couldn't talk to anyone else about it either, even though that would've been the right thing to do.

My mom noticed my moody behaviour and would often enter my bedroom to talk to me. I always said that I was okay when I really wasn't. I shrugged her off many times, but she wasn't a fool and she always kept coming back because she was worried about me.

"You'll make new friends in your new courses Danny, don't worry," she would often say to encourage me.

Her words turned out to be true when I met a pair of likeminded individuals in one of my Canadian history lectures during my second year of college. We were assigned a group project by our professor, and that's when I first met Sylvia and James. We started out as group members but ended up becoming the closest of friends as the months passed by. The biggest change for me was learning how to trust people again, which was difficult at first but something that I relearned.

Both Sylvia and James were always open and transparent with me, which I appreciated more than anything. I knew that they were humble and would never be the type to talk behind someone's back. We remained great friends for the entire academic year and in the following summer, we all agreed to go on a road trip together for a few days to New York City.

We were adventurous and we felt like it was the best place to visit at the time. It wasn't too close to where we lived in Brampton and Mississauga, but it wasn't a continent away from us either. I could never have imagined that I would travel anywhere like this, especially with friends that I made at school. Yet here I was, living my life with some amazing people by my side.

"This seems to be one of your happiest memories," Peri says. "Look at how ecstatic you all look compared to what we saw earlier."

"Sylvia was one of the brightest students I ever met, and James always kept it real," I say. "We sort of became our own version of the three musketeers."

It's something that I had longed for, especially after how Mike, Harold, and Sophie treated me. Having friends that unconditionally support you is a thing of beauty that many people take for granted all too often.

"They helped pick you up from the bottom and brought you back up to your feet," Peri says.

Amid the thousands of voices flying around Times Square, I'm dialed in on the trio in front of me. Past Danny stops taking pictures for a moment and speaks to Sylvia and James.

"We have to try out the pizza place that I was talking about earlier. It's right over there," Past Danny says as he points to a pizzeria close by.

"Oh my God, yes let's go please! I'm so hungry!" Sylvia says.

"Are we headed to the Empire State or Central Park after that?" James asks. "We still have some time to kill before we gotta head over to Yankee Stadium. The game starts at 7."

Past Danny and Sylvia both shout opposing answers and everyone starts laughing.

It's a moment of pure bliss that I'm witnessing. No aggressiveness, no arguments, and no hostility. Just a bunch of friends having a blast together and enjoying their lives to the fullest. If only all days could be like this one.

The trio leaves the red steps behind and begin to walk over to the pizzeria. Peri and I follow closely behind them as I continue to revel in all the memories I've reacquired.

"This was my very first road trip," I tell Peri. "I never even travelled this far with my own parents."

"Life's all about creating new and rewarding experiences, along with finding the right people to enjoy them with," Peri says.

I observe the sea of strangers all around us. There's so many people laughing, conversating, enjoying street performances, eating food, and taking pictures underneath the flashing billboards. Every single person here has a different story to tell. They each have their own unique version of what happiness means to them.

The trio in front of me are living out their own version of happiness, even if it's something as small as eating a slice of pizza together. All three of them stop walking and stand outside the pizzeria entrance. I move in closer to listen in on their conversation again.

My past self is standing in front of me with an endless smile on his face as he addresses his friends. "I've heard nothing but good things about this place. Let's see if their New York pepperoni special is worth the hype."

"I'm ready to pig out! The next time we eat will probably be at the stadium," James says.

"I can't wait for the game, we ended up getting some incredible seats. Right behind the dugout," Sylvia says.

"Trust me, it's going to be so different from a home game in Toronto," James replies.

A brief thought crosses my mind about how I was never able to go to a baseball game because my dad refused to take me as a kid. I refrain from expanding on that thought any further and my mind switches gears. The overwhelming sense of positivity I'm feeling in this moment is too great to let any negativity break through.

"I'm glad we were able to make this trip work and drive down here. There's so much to see," Past Danny says.

Peri looks over at me like a teacher checking up on his student. "You found a much better group of people to start a friendship with than those three bullies from before," Peri says. "Imagine if you stayed isolated and unapproachable after that fight. You wouldn't have met these two and you wouldn't have experienced these precious moments with them."

"I guess you're right," I say. "I got into this pessimistic mindset thinking that if all good things come to an end, then what's the point of even trying in the first place?"

"It's never really about the destination or the end result. What matters most is the journey that takes you there," Peri says.

I can't help but think of all the short-lived friend circles I was in and out of until this point. All those times I tried to fit in where I didn't belong. Those relations are always temporary without any real foundation.

All the "friends" who used me for their own benefit, tried to peer pressure me into doing things that I didn't want to, or contacted me only when they needed a favour. It takes a toll on you but once you finally discover a healthy friend circle, it changes everything and it can work wonders on your life.

I'm glad I found Sylvia and James when I did. Our paths couldn't have crossed at a better time when I needed respectable friends the most. I halt my thoughts for now and focus back on the trio as they're walking toward the pizzeria door.

"…I would be Wonder Woman," Sylvia says.

"Then I call Batman," James says while smirking.

"That means I'm Superman, even though he's a bit overpowered," Past Danny says.

It seems like this group could talk about anything in the world and never grow tired of one another. They're all smiling and laughing, making me feel delighted inside.

"Let's head on in," Past Danny says. "I can't wait any longer."

He opens the door and holds it open for Sylvia and James. I can see them getting excited as the delicious smell hits their noses. They enter the pizzeria and Past Danny follows as the door closes behind him.

I decide to follow the group in but as soon as I open the door, there's nothing behind it to my surprise. No chairs, no tables, no servers, no pizza. Nothing but a bright white light shining out of it that's impossible for me to see through. I close the door and turn my attention to Peri standing behind me.

"Wait, where'd they go? That's it? I wanted to see more," I say. I'm slightly disappointed at how much shorter this memory felt.

"Unfortunately, that's the end of this one Danny," Peri says. "You've seen what you needed to see, felt what you needed to feel, and regained your former memories in the process. We're able to move on now."

The emotional part of me wishes that I could stay here and remain in Sylvia and James' company again. I know that this isn't a real place with real people, but I still wouldn't mind reliving that comfort again. The logical part of me kicks in, telling me to stay focused and keep pushing on with my journey. I'm thankful for this pleasurable experience but I still have to figure out this mystery and go back to where I came from.

"If only I could relive this trip all over again, from the very beginning to the end," I say. "It was one of the most fun times in my entire life. But anyway, thank you for showing this to me. I'm ready to go now."

"Whenever there are bad times, good times are surely to follow. This was one of those very good times. After you," Peri says. He directs me to the pizzeria door, which is now our portal out of here and back to the undesirable forest.

I take a moment to view the entire square one last time. What a visual feast it is. I hope to visit it again one day if I ever survive my current predicament.

I turn around and face the same door that my past self, Sylvia, and James walked through. I stand tall and confident like I've taken notes from my past self. I grasp the metallic door handle of the pizzeria and gently open it. A bright white light shines upon me like it did in the arcade and Mr. Baker's guidance office.

"Here we go," I say. I walk into the doorframe and instantly become engulfed in the light's warm sensation.

Everything fades away as Peri closes the door behind him. The flashing lights and billboards are no longer present. The loud noises from the taxicab honks to the pedestrians' voices are now silenced.

There's only this soothing bright light that surrounds me now. I close my eyes without any visuals or sounds to distract me and I enjoy this temporary peace.

DOOR FOUR

THE DEPTHS

Wind streams across my face and I hear tree branches swaying back and forth. I sense that the white light is gone, and I open my eyes to see that we've made it back to home base. The clearing amid the dark forest is still intact. The third door has vanished, and four doors remain to be explored.

There's something else that requires my attention. The mysterious fog that I saw a while back is not only drawing closer to our position but also starting to encircle us. The crows that were once far away in the distance are moving up and becoming much louder above the fog. They appear more menacing and present an ominous warning to me.

"Tell me what it means," I say to Peri. I direct my hands at the fog that's slowly making its way around the clearing, patiently ensnaring us in a trap. "Look at how close it's gotten."

Peri doesn't seem bothered by it. "Take it as a signal for us to move quicker," he says.

"That's all? You've been with me this entire time and you know I'm moving as fast as I can," I say.

I grow weary of the ongoing secrecy. Peri can't keep avoiding me like this, so I stand my ground.

"I see what you're trying to show me, but what are you really trying to *do* for me?" I ask with a stern look on my face. "These doors show me a negative memory from my past, and then you show me a positive one that follows it. But what does any of that have to do with where I am now? Why can't I remember anything beyond what's shown in these memories?"

Peri stares at me for a while before finally speaking.

"We should keep moving Danny. There are still four doors left," Peri says.

That's not good enough and I need to know what's happening. Peri's going to have to be more convincing than that.

"I'm not moving from here until you give me some more information," I say.

I can tell that Peri doesn't want to break down the full scenario for me, but I need this cleared up for my remaining sanity.

Peri sighs before addressing me.

"You made a mistake that landed you here. Until you don't overcome this trial, that mistake may end up costing you your freedom from this place. As for that approaching fog that you keep noticing. It's been moving toward you since you first entered this forest. Once it reaches you inside of this clearing, you won't be able to open any more doors. You'll be stuck here. That's why I keep telling you to move faster before that happens."

I don't like the sound of any of that. I begin to think as hard as I can about this "mistake" I could've made. I try to recall any possible clues that may help me solve this mystery. How did I get here? Dark sky, water, shore, television, games, desk, paper, office, field, bicycle, billboards, pizza… this isn't working at all. I'm just picturing all the stuff that I saw from the three doors so far. What did Peri mean when he said that I'll be stuck here? I cover up my fear by asking some more probing questions.

"What's your story?" I ask. "You know a lot about me, but I don't know anything about you."

Peri stares at me with an unconvincing look on his face.

"Why are your shoes, pants, and shirt all black? Why do you really keep that knife on you? Why can't you tell me how I ended up here? Who are you really and what's your real name?"

I'm hurling questions at Peri as if I'm trying my best to see what sticks, but it doesn't phase him at all.

"Knowing the answers to these questions won't provide you with any sense of comfort, if that's what you're looking for," Peri says. "Continue on with your task and you'll get an idea of who I am by the end of this. You have my word Danny."

Taking a stranger's word is as good as taking no one's at all. Relying on Peri for answers isn't getting me anywhere, it's only slowing me down. If that incoming fog is really a danger to me, then there's nothing else to do but to push onward.

The constant darkness around me, that's now being blended with the fog and disturbing crows overhead, makes me uncomfortable. I would gladly trade these moody creatures and this haunted scenery for some gentler birds and a bright blue sky.

I walk over to the fourth door. It has a slight glow around it while the remaining doors are dormant and lifeless. My stomach churns as I try my best to predict all the possibilities that could be behind this door.

What else could have happened in my life that I need to learn something from? What is the mistake that landed me here? I've regained 20 years' worth of memories so far after that last door. That leaves me with 12 years to catch up to my current age. My attempts at guessing any possibilities of what happened within that time span are futile.

The unpredictability of this entire "trial," as Peri keeps mentioning, is starting to mess with my head. Who knows what lays waiting behind the remaining four doors? The bad memories could become much worse, and I don't know if I'm ready to experience that.

I'm frightened but I try not to show it. I stand tall and keep my head held high, awaiting to see what happens next. My hand draws closer to the brass doorknob and I grip it firmly. I open the door, step inside, and remain in place as the black void of this cold space consumes me. Peri follows and closes the door behind him, sealing the seam and closing off the only source of light.

I stand still in the darkness, awaiting the new environment to take shape by the glimmer. Once it arrives and starts creating, I pace around and wonder about where I'm headed next. After a few moments, I get an idea of the environment being made and I begin to chuckle. This is either pure coincidence or a joke intending to mock me.

I'm standing on a walking path with a lakeshore nearby, accompanied by a blue sky and calm birds chirping above me.

There are a ton of vibrant trees aligned on both sides of this walking path, which add a lot of depth to the scenery. This has to be some time in the fall season, as plenty of red, orange, and yellow leaves adorn their branches.

Peri and I observe every angle and become acquainted with the natural beauty before us. We begin walking along the path that's built parallel to the lakeshore on our right side. This environment is the most stunning and visually pleasing one yet.

I'm mesmerized by all trees lined up along the walking path as their leaves look like bright beacons filled with fiery colours. I remember that when I was growing up, fall, or autumn as others called it, had always been my favourite season. It was one thing to watch the leaves grow and turn green in the spring after a long winter, but I found it much more joyful to watch them transform into vivid colours in the fall after summer. The weather also became cooler around that time in September and October, which always made me excited to wear my favourite sweatshirts more often.

One of my favourite holidays was in the fall as well, being Halloween. Dressing up as someone much more interesting than myself for a day gave me the escape that I needed from my problems I had going on in my head. My mom would always buy me any costume that I wanted, and I remember dressing up as a firefighter, a werewolf, and various superheroes.

We'd cut up a pumpkin together, which was as orange as the leaves on the branches beside me, and turn it into a spooky jack-o'-lantern. My dad was obviously not a supporter of any of this, but we placed it out on the porch for Halloween evening anyway before my mom took me out for trick-or-treating. Whenever it fell on a weekday, she would take the afternoon shift off for me so I had a chance to go from house to house and collect as much candy as I could.

"Are you sure this is the right memory? I don't see anyone around here," I say to Peri as we're strolling along the path with no one in sight.

"It should be… Let's move a bit quicker and further up," Peri says. He holds up his left hand and snaps his fingers.

Something strange happens to my legs as I'm walking. They begin hovering above the ground and I start gliding instead!

"Well, this is new," I say while looking down at my new and improved mode of traversal.

"Your past self should be around here somewhere," Peri says as we're both gliding down the walking path at a much faster pace now.

Tree after tree passes us as we quickly whip by them. After about a minute or two, we see a figure jogging down the same path in front of us up ahead. There's also a long pier that's much further away and stretches far out into the lake beside us. There appears to be two people walking to the end of the pier but it's difficult to tell from the lengthy distance between us.

I forget about the pier for now and instead, focus my attention on the person that's running ahead. Peri and I swiftly glide over to this figure. I'm able to view his front side as I hover right beside him and keep up with his pace.

"Well then… that wasn't too hard. Here I am," I confirm to Peri. My past self, who appears to be slightly older here, is jogging down this scenic path while wearing his black running shoes, black shorts, and a grey sweatshirt. He has red headphones over his ears and is listening to music while zoned in on his cardiovascular exercise.

Peri and I glide down the path right behind Past Danny. I continue to take in the splendor of the natural vista surrounding me, as well as the peace and quiet of it all. The longer we follow Past Danny down the path, the more I'm curious about what could possibly happen next. My past self is working up a sweat and jogging at a steady pace while his music provides him with the motivation that he needs to keep going.

The long pier that I previously noticed is fast approaching on our right side now. I squint my eyes and I make out a lot more details compared to before. There's a wooden railing that acts as a border for the wooden pier underneath it, which extends a good distance out into the lake.

There are two people standing at the very edge of the pier, one much taller than the other. As the pier is almost perpendicular from our right side, I notice that the two figures are a young girl and an elderly woman.

The little girl is dressed up in an angel costume, with a pair of wings on her back and a small halo on top of her head. She's jumping up and down with excitement while the elderly woman is watching over her. Past Danny also notices the two individuals as he runs past the entrance of the pier. He briefly smiles at the sight of this enthusiastic girl in her tiny costume before continuing with his jog ahead.

There's no one else around besides Past Danny, the little girl, and the old woman. I start to develop an extremely bad feeling about all of this, especially after seeing the little girl so close to the water like that. I decide to do something that I haven't done before. I stop following Past Danny and I deviate from the path, gliding toward the pier instead.

"Danny, stay on course!" Peri yells out. I don't heed his advice and I glide all the way over to the edge of the pier where the two individuals are standing. I stop a few steps away from them and I observe their interaction with each other.

"Look grandma, I'm flying like an angel!" the young girl exclaims, as she carefully stands on one of the horizontal beams attached to the wooden railing. Her arms are spread apart as if the entirety of the lake in front of her is her personal kingdom.

"Get down Bella! It's not safe to do that," her grandma says, snapping her out of her excitement.

"No fair! First, I can't go trick-or-treating tonight with Peter and grandpa, and now you won't let me have any fun!" Bella responds in a high-pitched voice, along with a huge frown on her face. She crosses her arms out of frustration. She's an adorable child who deserves all the attention in the world.

"Bella don't say that. You know that Peter and grandpa love to walk fast with their longer legs. You can go with them next year when you're older," the grandma says. "For now, how does some ice cream sound?"

"Oh yay! I want chocolate vanilla fudge with peanuts on top please," Bella requests as she switches her frown to a grin.

"Yes ma'am," the grandma says. "Hold on, I'm getting a phone call from mommy."

She takes out a ringing cellphone from her bag and answers the call. I listen in on her conversation to pick up some potential clues.

"Hello! We're just by the lakeshore and about to get some ice cream now. We'll be home in about an hour dear," the grandma says.

The grandma continues talking casually and she looks out toward the endless lake for a moment.

"Yes, the view is wonderful from here. We should all come together next time. I'll show you the pictures we took when we come home," the grandma says.

As the grandma is wrapping up her conversation, I shift my focus over to Bella.

My heart instantly sinks to my stomach. Bella has climbed on the railing again but she's even higher than last time, standing on the uppermost part of it. Her grandma had been keeping a watchful eye over her until these few brief seconds.

As Bella's grandma ends the call and is placing the phone back into her bag, Bella spreads her arms wide apart and expresses her triumph.

"Grandma look, I told you I can fly!"

And then it happens. Bella loses her balance for only a second. She leans forward and flips over the railing, splashing down into the lake beneath her.

"BELLA NO!" her grandma screams, and she continues to shriek as loud as she can.

In the distance, Past Danny hears the grandma's cries as he's taking pictures of the lake with his cellphone close to the pier. He throws off his red headphones and begins to sprint toward my direction, but he's still far away and there's no time to lose.

The emotions of my past self hit my mind all at once and my panic levels skyrocket. More of my memories have been restored but there's no time to think about them. The adrenaline surges throughout my entire body. Instead of waiting for my past self to arrive, I decide to jump into the lake after Bella.

I sink as far down into the depths as I can. I see Bella at the bottom using all her strength to splash around in the cold water, frantically trying to resurface back to her grandma. I can hear her muffled cries for help as the water infiltrates her lungs, slowly drowning out the noise.

Down here, it's much darker as the bright blue sky is no longer present. I reach out to grab Bella's little arm, but it doesn't work. My translucent hand goes right through her flesh. I try again and it's the same result. I continue my attempts to make some sort of contact with Bella before it's too late.

Suddenly, I hear another splash of water above me. I quickly glide back up to the surface and hope for someone else to rescue this innocent angel.

It's Past Danny and he has his whole body submerged in the water, except for one arm that he's using to cling on to the railing.

"I'm sorry," Past Danny tells the grandma while shivering. "I tried reaching down for her, but I can't feel her. I can't go any lower, I can't swim."

"Bella!" the grandma yells with streams of tears running down her cheeks. Her continuous wailing echoes far and wide as she overlooks the railing where Bella was standing.

Past Danny pulls himself back on top of the pier to call an ambulance from his phone. While all that's happening, I glide back down into the deep water and try to save Bella once more. She's still flailing as much as she can, desperately trying to return to the surface.

I struggle to pick her up with my arms as they keep going right through her. I know that what I'm trying to do is useless but a part of me believes that I can somehow change this outcome.

As each second passes, the light in Bella's eyes diminishes. After a few more attempts that end in failure, I finally move back from her.

I stare at this poor soul dressed up in her angel costume with her wings and halo. Before Bella uses up her final gasps, it seems as if she's looking directly into my eyes. Is it a mere coincidence or can she somehow sense that I was trying to save her?

Her eyes gaze right into mine as her arms stop moving. Soon after, the light from her eyes is gone and her lifeless body remains still under the weight of the water. I know that there's nothing left to do at this point. I feel confused and my sadness is amplified to the stratosphere.

This is something that no one on the planet should ever have to see or experience for themselves. I take one last look at this angel before I hopelessly glide back to the surface.

I make it back on top of the pier, where a professional rescue diver is getting ready to plunge into the water and retrieve Bella's body. I don't have the desire to witness this play out any further, so I begin to walk away.

I make my way across the pier back to the shore, where bright red lights are flashing all over from multiple emergency vehicles that've showed up. It seems that the grandma has collapsed out of shock, as a few paramedics are carrying her on a stretcher before loading her into an ambulance.

Past Danny is sitting on a nearby bench with a towel over his shoulders, provided by one of the paramedics. He's being questioned about the incident that's taken place in front of him.

I feel what my past self is feeling in the moment, and it's the most horrible experience in this entire journey so far. My mind isn't functioning, my body's squeamish from the inside out, and my heart's been shattered into a million pieces. There's an overwhelming sensation of guilt that's taken a hold over me to my very core. It's like I murdered someone in broad daylight because of my inability to act and make a difference. As my anxiety and grief persists, Peri shows up beside me.

"I can't do this anymore. I can't experience stuff like this all over again," I say.

"What happened on this day by the lake wasn't your fault Danny," Peri replies. "It may not seem like it right now, but everything happens for a reason."

What's that supposed to mean? This was entirely my fault and no one else's. I have so many questions that require answers as a plethora of emotions are picking my mind apart.

If there's such a thing, why did God allow this poor little girl's life to be over so soon? Why are some good people punished early while some bad people get to enjoy a nice, long life? Why wasn't Bella allowed to grow any older and have fun in school, play with her friends, pursue her passions, get married one day, and at the very least, go trick-or-treating next Halloween? Why wasn't I able to save her from the cold clutches of death? What else could I have done differently to change the result? Why couldn't I have learned to swim before this happened? How does any of this make any sense? The questions keep running through my mind at light speed. Sadness, confusion, anger, fear, and most of all, regret, consume me.

Why am I alive and Bella isn't?

I remember that this was the most pressing question that plagued my mind for many months after this horrific incident. Day by day, the dark roots of my negative thoughts leeched the life out of me and absorbed my mind, like how plant roots absorb water. I was hurting on the inside, but I didn't want to tell anyone because I was fearful of transferring this remorseful and regretful burden over to them.

"You can't save everyone," Peri says. "Guilt can destroy a person from the inside out. The world works in mysterious ways, but it's the natural order of things. Life and death are two sides of the same coin."

"Are you saying that I was supposed to be completely fine with the way that little girl died? I'm supposed to believe in some sick and twisted version of 'fate'?" I snap at Peri, who seems to show no empathy.

"That's not what I'm saying," Peri says. "What I'm saying is that you can't torture yourself for things that aren't in your control Danny. Death is a part of everyone's life all around the world, from the most isolated islands to the busiest cities. From the naive young to the experienced middle-aged to the wise elders. No matter how soon or how late it happens, everyone must eventually perish."

It's difficult for me to comprehend this concept because I keep thinking about all the people who deserve to live a long life but are taken far too soon. It's a game that can't be won, but why do some people get to play it longer than others? The cycle of life and death is unfair and cruel.

I think about the people who heroically intervene in critical situations and manage to postpone someone's grim fate.

Meanwhile, others like me are a total failure and embarrassment under the same circumstances.

I remember that I had many sleepless nights after this incident. I would constantly lay awake in my bed and perpetually question my inability to act in the moment. When Bella sank to the depths of that lake, so did a piece of my soul.

I should've been able to save her. The issue that I blamed was when I was young, I had an extra muscle tissue in my right nostril that prevented me from breathing properly. Since my nostrils were only able to do half the work, I constantly had to keep my mouth open because that was the best way for oxygen to pass through.

I remember my mom once enrolled me in a swimming class when I was about 8 years old. I had a lot of trouble learning the simplest of fundamentals. I felt ashamed as the other kids watched me struggle in the pool so after a while, my mom withdrew me from the class.

A few years later when I was in middle school, I had that extra muscle tissue successfully removed with a surgery. However, I didn't show any interest in taking swimming lessons again until much later in my life, when I was in my fourth and final year of college. One day in September, I stopped by the front desk of the recreation centre to inquire about private swimming lessons. This was a few weeks after I turned 21 and college courses had begun. I wanted to sign up for an activity to occupy myself outside of my academic obligations.

The employee at the front desk told me that a couple of hour-long sessions would cost me hundreds of dollars, which I thought was far out of my budget. I also thought about how this expensive skill wouldn't really be worth it to me in the long run anyway. I had my student loans to worry about and learning how to swim wasn't a priority for me. I refrained from enrolling in those swimming lessons so that I could save my money and pay off my debt sooner.

I walked out of the recreation centre doors that day without a second thought. After what happened with Bella and throughout all my sleepless nights, I deeply wished that I had turned around that day and signed up for the swimming lessons. They would've better equipped me for this ordeal and the outcome could've been much different.

"I could've saved her," I say to Peri. "I was right there."

"You don't know that for sure," Peri says. "Do you think lifeguards, firefighters, or police officers are always able to save everyone in trouble?"

"No, but at least they're more prepared than I was," I say. "I let that poor girl and her grandma down. I know I could've done something else besides sway in the water like an idiot… Other than calling the paramedics, I was useless."

"You can spend the rest of your life debating what could've happened, should've happened, or would've happened, but you can't change the fact it *has* happened," Peri says.

I look at Past Danny sitting on the bench with his head down. The ambulance begins to pull away and leave the scene to head toward the hospital.

The same raw and untamed emotions he's feeling are flowing throughout me, as I once sat in shame on that exact same bench.

What started out as an ordinary day for a jog ended up being a traumatic event that changed my life forever.

The blue sky now represented the water that Bella drowned in. The red leaves on the trees now represented the blood on my hands. A white seagull flying far above me now represented an angel flying toward heaven. And if there's no heaven, then she surely experienced hell on earth at the bottom of that lake.

I'll never forget the costume she was wearing. It's safe to say that I never celebrated or enjoyed Halloween again.

"You simply can't change the outcome sometimes, no matter how hard you try," Peri says. "You have to learn to accept it and move forward."

"It's much easier said than done," I say. "You don't know how hard it is until you're thrown into a situation like that."

This entire memory sequence is the absolute worst of nightmares that I never wanted to relive, experience, or remember in any way whatsoever. The beautiful landscape no longer retains its original beauty and I feel changed from within. I would've been much better off not having this missing memory restored to my mind at all. I can't take this torment any longer and I know that Peri sees the grueling sorrow on my face.

"Let's move on then," Peri says. He raises his right hand up in front of him. Peri snaps his fingers and finally rids us of this appalling place.

The environment disintegrates before my eyes but remains engrained within my mind. Everything fades to pitch black for a moment like the previous three doors. The glimmer then begins to construct a new environment and I have no idea what to expect. Anywhere would be better than here, but what could've possibly made me feel any better after witnessing this tragedy?

The blue sky has shifted into white fluorescent lights above me. The wide jogging path is now a narrow hallway in front of me, with several doors on each side. This place has the feel of a doctor's office or a hospital to it. Once the environment has been filled up with colour, Peri and I walk around it to gain our footing.

My initial reaction is to open one of the doors on either side of us, as the memory I need to view may be taking place behind it. The first doorknob doesn't budge, so I try the next one. It also doesn't move.

I end up trying to open all the doors in this claustrophobic hallway, but all of them are closed. This reminds me of the doors from the forest and I'm forced to seek an alternative. Behind me, there seems to be a dead end as the hallway doesn't lead to any other area or rooms. In front of me, however, there's a connecting hallway that leads somewhere else. I nod my head at Peri to let him know where I'm going before I begin to march forward.

Once I make it to the end of the hallway, I make a sharp left around the corner and view a new area that's much larger than I expected. It's a waiting lobby that contains a ton of empty seats, along with a front desk and a young receptionist sitting behind it. There are a few people sitting down in their seats, but I don't see myself among them as I walk by. Across from the front desk, there's a sturdy revolving door and a big welcome sign that has

Toronto Children's Hospital written on it. What would I possibly be doing here?

"Where's my past self?" I ask Peri.

"You'll have to wait and see what happens," Peri says while casually pacing around.

I walk around the lobby to try to find some clues as to what may occur in the coming moments. There's a small family sitting down a few steps away from the revolving door and I can overhear them speaking to each other.

"Will the doctor fix me today mommy?" a little boy asks while holding his brown teddy bear by his side.

His mom looks at him as if she's trying to hold back a tear before replying with, "Yes honey, he will."

"The results will be better than last time, don't worry," the dad whispers to her.

Is this place supposed to make me feel better or worse? Everything is reminding me of Bella and I'm not sure if that's what Peri was intending.

I walk away from this family because I don't want to feel more down than I already am. I come across a wall next to the front desk that's been entirely used as a background for countless paintings. It's filled up with cheerful, hopeful, and colourful illustrations of all shapes and sizes. There's no space left untouched, and it makes the rest of the hospital walls look bland in comparison. There are tons of hand-painted animals, rainbows, flowers, trees, and people holding hands. I'm assuming these drawings were created by children, so they're not exactly proportionate but that's what makes them unique and perfect.

I enjoy viewing a masterpiece depicting an elephant with a tiny head and an extremely long trunk that's holding out a bouquet of sunflowers for a zebra in the middle of a jungle.

"Kids have the best imagination," I say to Peri, trying to take my mind off Bella and avoid the guilt that's weighing me down. "Wouldn't you say?" I ask as Peri's unresponsive.

"Yeah. They are… creative," Peri responds while looking zoned out. Something seems off about him in this specific environment, more than anywhere else we've been so far.

"Is there something wrong?" I ask.

"Nothing's wrong Danny. Hospitals can be a strenuous place for me," Peri says. "These are great paintings."

I wonder what he means by that because this is new to me. It's the first time that Peri's shown any sort of emotion toward an environment at all.

I'm curious about Peri's thoughts on hospitals but I can relate to his general dislike for them. Whenever I had to visit a doctor's office or a hospital as a kid, I would always feel cold and empty inside. I knew that they could be places of great excitement and celebration, but also places of great suffering and sadness. A newborn baby will light up a couple's world whereas the untimely passing of a parent will destroy a child's world. I don't pay this thought any more mind because I've had enough of death for one day.

I continue my stroll around the lobby while analyzing more paintings on the wall. As I'm viewing a lion running across a rainbow, I hear the revolving door spinning from the entrance. Someone's entering the lobby, so I turn my attention toward the approaching figure and walk right over. Within a few seconds, I confirm it's who we've been looking for.

My past self has walked into the place, whose face has slightly matured since the lakeshore incident. In this memory, Past Danny is dressed in casual attire. A pair of white shoes, dark blue jeans, white t-shirt, and a Toronto Blue Jays cap on his head. He has a stubble beard on his face that's similar to mine but looks more like a prototype version of it. He's holding a large cardboard box with both of his arms out in front of him.

I walk behind my past self as he approaches the front desk. This feels like such a surreal experience to me, being able to witness my younger body moving around like this right in front of my eyes. It's like looking at a stranger and a friend at the same time. It's hard to believe that this was once me, existing as a physical manifestation within the real world.

What am I doing here in this children's hospital out of all places? Why am I alone and what am I holding in the box? I have many new questions, but I know that there's no point of dwelling on them for too long. I'll have to wait to find out.

Past Danny begins to smile as he arrives at the front desk and greets the receptionist.

"Jessica! How are you doing?" Past Danny asks her.

"Hey Danny, I'm good! It's so nice to see you again. How've you been?" she asks.

"Can't complain. I was out running some errands, so I thought I'd stop by. It's really nice outside," Past Danny says.

"How cute! I wish I was out enjoying the sunshine too. I'm stuck here on a Friday evening instead," Jessica says with a small frown.

"You can still catch a few hours of it if you're done work soon," Danny says.

I notice Past Danny's watch on his wrist as he continues to hold up the cardboard box. It's the same vintage watch that I'm currently wearing on my own wrist. It's displaying 7:10 p.m., so I'm guessing this memory may be taking place some time in the summer when the sunshine doesn't fade away until shortly after 9 p.m.

"I'm done at 11 tonight so I'll have to wait," Jessica says. "But I'm glad you stopped by! You haven't been around in a few weeks."

"I know, I'm sorry. I got caught up studying for my summer school exams," Past Danny says.

"Oh right, how'd they go? My last one is this Monday," Jessica says.

"I think I did pretty good. Once the final grades are up, we can finally graduate," Past Danny says.

If Past Danny is talking about graduating from college after summer school, then I'd be almost 22 years old here.

"We have to celebrate once we do! What were you studying again?" Jessica asks.

"World history with a minor in religion," Past Danny says.

"That's exciting! I always wanted to take more courses like that. I feel like I've looked at enough humans from a biological level, but nothing from a historical or social level," Jessica says.

"Here's a mini lesson for free. Have you ever heard of Zoroastrianism? From ancient Persia?" Past Danny asks.

"No, what's that? Sounds cool and mystical," Jessica says.

"So basically, it's one of the oldest religions in the world, and could also be the oldest monotheistic faith," Past Danny explains. "I won't get into specifics, but this religion references a concept called 'dualism' or in other words, the ongoing battle between good and evil."

"Clearly my flirting skills needed some improvement here," I say to Peri while my past self continues to talk to Jessica in the background.

"Hey, it's good information. Plus, she seems to be really enjoying it," Peri says.

"Yeah right," I say. "She'd rather watch those animal paintings dry on the walls."

"Look at her, she can't take her eyes off you," Peri says.

He doesn't seem to be wrong, as Jessica continuously stares at my past self with much interest while he elaborates on his story.

"…so, you have *cosmic* dualism dealing with good and evil within the universe, and you have *moral* dualism dealing with good and evil within our own minds. The second one is more about free will and how you're able to choose to be happy or sad in response to your circumstances," Past Danny continues. He then realizes he's talking too much and decides to conclude his history lesson. "Anyway, if you're interested, I can send you my final paper if you want to read it," Past Danny says. "You'll get a better idea of what I'm talking about."

"You really have a passion for this stuff and it shows Danny! And for sure, send it to my email, I'd love to read it," Jessica says with a smile.

Jessica then glances at the cardboard box in Past Danny's arms.

"By the way, the kids absolutely loved your donations the last time you came. Annie hasn't put that book down for a day yet. You really didn't have to bring any more stuff!" Jessica says.

"It's the least I can do. I was cleaning my basement with my mom over the weekend, and I found more of my old toys and books. If I didn't bring them here, she would've donated them to the thrift store near our house."

"You're so kind! Did you want to leave the box here or did you want to take it up?" Jessica asks.

"I'd love to take it up today if that's okay," Past Danny says.

"Yeah of course! Fill out the visitor log and you're all good to go," Jessica says.

"Which room is Annie in again? I'll visit her first and ask her about that book she's been reading," Past Danny says as he places the box on the ground and signs the visitor log with a pen.

"She's in room 1213. She's going to be so happy to see you," Jessica says.

"Thanks Jessica, I'll catch you soon," Past Danny says with a smile. He picks up the box and begins to turn away from the front desk.

"Bye Danny, have fun!" Jessica says to him while smiling back.

"Well, she's a very nice girl," Peri says as we start walking behind my past self.

"I met her in one of my college classes, close to the end of my third year. We clicked right away but we never really spent any time together," I say.

Peri doesn't say anything back and simply smiles in return.

We follow my past self to some elevator doors. He balances the box with his arms and pushes the button with a bolded arrow pointing up. The elevator doors open immediately. Peri and I walk in with Past Danny, and he presses the button with the number twelve on it.

"How are you feeling?" Peri asks as we begin moving up.

"I don't know, nervous and eager at the same time. I'm not sure when this memory is taking place. The trigger hasn't happened yet, so I don't know what to expect," I say.

"A piece of advice is that you should always expect the unexpected. That way, you won't be caught off guard as easily," Peri says.

"Are you saying I'm supposed to expect bad things to happen all the time? Live a life of me constantly trying to save myself from disappointment?" I ask.

"No, but start picturing your life as a car travelling down a winding road, with many twists and turns along the way," Peri says. "There may be other people who travel down straighter, safer, and securer roads, but yours is not one of them."

I don't pay much attention to his car example because I have my own analogy. A movie is playing in front of my eyes because it appears to be reality when it's not. All I know about this movie is that I'm the main character who's aimlessly wandering around from scene to scene. I don't know who's directing this thing or who's pulling all the strings. I don't even know what role Peri is playing in all of this. Is he really some sort of sidekick or is he secretly the villain?

Deep down, I'm still thinking about Bella's final glance at me when she was at the bottom of the lake. I find it hard to believe that I would've forgotten about her and moved on so soon. If the trend holds true, then wherever this elevator takes me will assist me in mending my guilt-ridden mindset. My mom, Mr. Baker, Sylvia, and James helped me within the previous doors, so I keep that hope alive and anticipate what's to come.

I hear the elevator chime go off as its doors slide open on the twelfth floor. Past Danny exits and turns left, walking ahead of us and passing door after door.

1201

1203

1205

1207

We continue walking down the hallway until we stop at the door labelled *1213*. Past Danny gently opens the door, only to be greeted with a huge gasp from a little girl sitting in her bed.

"DANNY!" she exclaims.

"Hey Annie, how've you been?" Past Danny asks with a grin as he enters the room.

Peri and I follow him inside.

This room is pretty cramped, only big enough for a single bed and a bit of extra standing room. There's a small television in front of the bed and a window on its left-hand side, which is where we choose to stand.

Annie seems to be the most adorable little girl, with a purple bandana on her head and a soft, blue blanket beside her. She gives Past Danny a hug as he sits on the bed right next to her.

"I'm okay. I haven't had any visitors in while, other than the nurse and Jessica," Annie says.

"That's alright, as long as you're comfortable here. Hey, I brought you some more stuff I think you'll enjoy," Past Danny says.

"I'm still reading that book you brought last time, the one with the small man who travels with a bunch of dwarves to kill a dragon!" Annie says.

"That one's of my favourites, I'm glad you like it!" Past Danny says.

All at once, the emotions and memories hit my mind like a pile of bricks. Suddenly, I go from feeling guilty, down, and defeated to feeling fulfilled, thankful, hopeful, and most of all, happy. I'm experiencing the same emotions as Past Danny right here in this very moment. I feel what I once felt when I visited Annie in her hospital room, who was all alone with no immediate family to keep her company. It's an overwhelming feeling and I stumble a bit before Peri puts an arm on my shoulder and helps me regain my balance.

Past Danny opens the box he brought from home, and Annie starts clapping.

"I have a stuffed elephant and some more books for you. You'll like this one for sure. It's about a boy who goes to a magical school and learns to become a wizard," Past Danny says.

"Thank you so much Danny!" Annie says and excitedly lunges forward to hug him again.

With more of my memories restored, I remember all my interactions with Annie as she continues to catch up with Past Danny in the background. I recall that this particular memory is about three weeks prior to turning 22 and finding out that I'd be officially graduating from college once my summer school grades were in. It's also about ten months after the incident with Bella at the pier.

I'm not sure how this is happening in my translucent state, but a bittersweet tear rolls down my cheek. While I'm delighted to experience this memory again, I remember attending Annie's funeral a few months from now.

Annie lived a life filled with energy and excitement but unfortunately, she suffered from leukemia and wasn't destined to live a very long one.

When Bella passed away, the time that followed was extremely difficult for me because my self-blame felt eternal. I knew I had to do or find something that filled some joy in me again, otherwise my mind wouldn't last much longer. One night, I looked up a children's hospital online and while I didn't live too close to it, I decided that I would drive down at least once a month to help in any way that I could.

I started to donate many old items from my house to as many children as I could. Throughout those brief interactions with other children in the hospital, I met so many wonderful souls. Most of them wouldn't go on and live long enough to experience their teenage years. Annie was one of those children who developed a special place in my heart because despite her circumstances, she displayed endless enthusiasm. The memories we created together before her death were priceless and timeless.

This children's hospital instilled a sense of maturity within me. All those recurring trips helped me realize that I truly didn't have the power to save everyone, which is what Peri was explaining to me at the shore. What I *did* have the power to do was help these children make the most of their remaining time here on this earth with lots of laughs, cheers, thrills, and fun.

My soul had hit absolute rock bottom, but it also became elevated to the peak of a mountain within that time frame. The happiness I felt was insurmountable whenever I saw those kids' faces light up like a Christmas tree after donating one of my old toys or books to them. The smallest of gestures can go a long way in making someone else's day.

"Thank you for showing me this," I say to Peri. "These moments really helped me move on, especially when I thought all my hope was lost."

"Every one of those children were grateful for what you did for them," Peri says. "You may not have been able to save their physical bodies, but you helped save their minds."

I remain silent and think about Bella again.

"I'm sorry you had to experience that trauma by the pier," Peri continues. "You weren't able to save Bella, but believe me, you helped save the kids here in another way."

I take a deep breath and sigh.

"I felt like I had a real purpose for the first time in a long time," I say.

By committing myself to making a small difference at this children's hospital, I remember how the roots of my negative thoughts were finally sheared. I stopped blaming myself constantly and my conscience became free. The truth is that these kids helped save *me*, more than they'll ever know.

Past Danny and Annie are playing a board game with each other, laughing their Friday summer evening away in this confined hospital room. Another tear rolls down my cheek and Peri notices this one before I wipe it away. I was always the type of person who never liked showing others his emotions.

"Not all tears are bad, but an old saying comes to mind. *Don't cry because it's over, smile because it happened,*" Peri says.

I never really wore my heart on my sleeve as often as I should've, but this entire trip down memory lane is slowly opening me up to some change. I agree with Peri's statement, so I express a small smile.

I turn around and look out of the window. Beyond the hundreds of buildings visible in downtown Toronto, there's a beautiful sunset to behold that's dipping down across the lake.

I can't help but wonder about all the people in the world whose minds may be poisoned by their own guilt and regret. There could be millions of people out there who experienced a similar fate but instead of helping themselves, they end up harming themselves when they can't handle the grief anymore.

I think about all the people out there who are simply unable to recover from the heavy burdens they voluntarily carry on their backs, with no one else to relieve them of their self-imposed punishment. I truly feel for these people because that easily could've been me.

I was unable to jump over the tall hurdle placed in front of me. Only with the help of others, like Annie, was I was able to overcome that barrier and take myself out of that negative mindset. If I hadn't attempted to make this small change in my life, I would've continued to mope around in my bedroom and wish that I were at the bottom of that lake instead of Bella. This one change shifted my entire perspective on life and what it meant to be alive.

I snap myself out of my thoughts and turn back around to look at Past Danny and Annie in their blissful state.

"You let me win!" Annie says.

"I did not, you totally beat me!" Past Danny replies. "Good game. Now, do you want to watch a movie while I visit the other kids? You gotta watch the one I was telling you about, the one with the green ogre who lives in a swamp."

"Ew, sounds gross but I'll watch it!" Annie says.

As Past Danny gets up from Annie's bed, her warm eyes turn cold and her contagious smile disappears.

"How much longer do you think I have Danny?" Annie asks in a quieter tone with her head drooping down.

It pains me to see her like this because she's fully aware of the position she's in. It's something that no one should ever have to experience: knowing you don't have long to live and awaiting your impending doom. Every passing date on the calendar must feel like death is taking one step closer toward your home. You won't know for sure when it'll arrive at your doorstep, but it'll inevitably barge through your front door to take you away.

"Don't worry Annie, your treatments are going to make you better and you'll be okay," Past Danny reassures her. "You're a strong warrior!"

"Like one of the dwarves who fight the dragon?" Annie asks while raising her head.

"Even stronger," Past Danny says.

"Will you come visit more often?" Annie asks as her excitement returns to her.

"Of course I will. I'm going to do whatever I can to make you happy," Past Danny says with a smile. "And don't forget, you still have much to live for Annie… you still have much to live for."

Annie lunges to hug him and says, "Thank you."

I take a deep breath and sigh once more, remembering that I started visiting Annie more for the next three months before she passed away.

"You're a good man," Peri says. "A man who knows what compassion is and has a depth of feeling for those around him."

"I really tried," I say. I can't take my eyes off Annie and her innocence.

"Don't ever think that you didn't do enough. Believe me, just *trying* to do some good in this world and keeping your head up is enough. There are so many people out there who won't even try. They'll give up right away as soon as they fail at something. Picking yourself up after being knocked down is what defines you Danny. Simply trying goes a long way," Peri says.

I nod in acknowledgement, and I feel a sense of pride knowing I played an important role in helping Annie live the most of her life with the time that she had left. In some ways, I feel like I redeemed myself for my failure to do the same with Bella.

"I'll be back Annie, I'm going to visit the other kids down the hall," Past Danny says.

"Okay! I'll start that ogre movie you recommended," Annie says.

Peri and I watch my past self walk out of the room as the door slowly closes. Before it's completely shut, I catch a glimpse of Past Danny walking over to the room right across from this one, on his way to make another child's day. Right when the door is closed, a bright light shines through from the opening at the bottom.

I look over at Peri. "I guess that's it then."

"The lesson is taught, and the memory is complete," Peri says. "We're ready to move on."

I look at Annie one last time, knowing that I won't ever have this chance again. She places her new book on the bedside table and snuggles underneath her blanket with her new plush elephant. She scrolls through a couple of screens on the television in front of her and starts the movie, all ready to enjoy the show.

"Take care Annie. I'll see you again one day," I quietly say with a smile.

I turn toward the door, take a deep breath, grasp the doorknob, and open it wide. The hallway that Peri and I walked through is no more and the bright light penetrates my eyes.

I take a few steps into the warm light and my body becomes engulfed by its radiance. Peri follows and gently closes the door behind him. The children's hospital disappears into nothingness while the new memories my mind has acquired become solidified. I don't feel as tormented anymore because of my renewed sense of hope. The tragedy with Bella led my mind to shackles, but the lessons with Annie pushed my mind to liberation.

THE BOTTLE

My body and my mind feel heavier but more fulfilled since I first started this journey. All my recollections are gradually weighing me down yet empowering me to push forward to the end. When I first awoke in the shallow water and made my way to shore, I was a blank canvas. An empty book with no words. With each memory I've regained since, progress has been made to restore my mind to what it once was.

Without memories, what good is a brain to a human body? How must people cope with their lives when they suffer from some type of memory loss? Where and how do you begin to pick up the fragmented pieces of your life?

It would feel like you spent your entire life completing a jigsaw puzzle but one day, something unfortunate happens and it gets destroyed within seconds, forcing you to start all over. I have a whole new perspective on what it means to appreciate one's memories and thoughts. While I continue to try to remember what got me here in the first place, I'm grateful to have recovered many of my memories since childhood.

I look around the clearing I'm standing in and it's become significantly smaller in my absence. The piece of land where the first door once stood has been intruded by the fog that's now occupying that space. Peri and I have been gone longer than expected with the last door. The fog has not only encircled us at this point but has also started to creep inward.

This clearing within the dark forest is no longer safe and we're enclosed right in it. The thick fog is acting as a border around us to prevent any retreat. The crows, coloured as dark as the night sky, are flying above the fog and cawing as loud as ever. Time is now my real enemy and each second that passes here is an advantage for this invading threat.

"Peri!?" I yell.

"I'm here," Peri says, walking up from behind me. "Are you alright?"

"I'm fine but look at this," I say while pointing around us. "How do we stop it?"

"We keep moving Danny," Peri says.

"All this jumping through time is starting to take a toll on me," I say. "Is there honestly no other way?"

"Do you wish to remain stuck here?" Peri asks.

"What do you mean by 'stuck'?" I snap back. "You still haven't told me anything about where I am, what I'm doing, or where I'm going!"

"Stuck as in you not being able to return to where you come from," Peri replies while staring at me. "I've already told you this before."

"Why are you acting like we're on Mars or something?" I ask with a raised tone. "What is it that you're hiding from me?"

"It's not about hiding anything. This isn't my doing… It's about bringing you back to the light. I'm not only here to help you as a messenger, but as a friend. This fog will consume you once it's too late. Focus on the remaining doors because it's your only chance to avoid that."

My hands clench up into fists, which I then place on my forehead while letting out a groan. I don't know what to think anymore and I don't know what to say.

Peri breaks up the lingering silence.

"I know I've shown you a lot of bad memories so far. But you've seen how there's just as many good memories to appreciate in hindsight. We don't spend enough time recognizing the many positive things that happen in our lives, no matter how big or how small they are. People tend to focus on the negative things that distract them from enjoying their lives and living them to the fullest."

"It's because the negative things are harder to get over," I say. "Some of those moments can break you down from the inside out. Who are you to decide what deserves more focus and what doesn't?"

"No matter how difficult it seems, we have to persevere through the dark times," Peri says. "There's *always* light at the end of the tunnel."

He pauses for a moment as we compose ourselves.

"These next three doors could be your toughest yet. You'll need to be strong once those hurtful memories begin to enter your mind," Peri says.

I don't like the sound of that, but I try to shrug it off as best as I can. "I'll be able to handle them, don't worry about me," I say.

"Remember, for every negative memory, there's a positive one waiting on the other side," Peri says. "For every bad parent, there's someone out there who genuinely cares about you. For every bad teacher, there's another who will bring out your potential. For every bad friend, there's a few more that will have your back. For every time we feel guilt, there's always an opportunity to redeem ourselves."

I know that Peri is speaking the truth but there's a part of me that's finding it hard to accept. Hurtful memories may eventually be overcome, but they remain imprinted within your heart and in your mind forever. They're never truly gone, no matter how much time passes by. The most difficult part is learning to live with them.

I view the fog surrounding us from all directions, which jolts my focus back to the door.

"Come on then, let's go," I say.

We walk to the fifth door and I try to analyze it as if it's going to spit some clue at me for what's to come. The wooden surface and brass doorknob are glowing, inviting me inside. Under my breath, I whisper all the places I've seen so far and try my best to predict what could be next.

Living room, arcade, classroom, office, baseball diamond, Times Square, lakeshore, hospital… What else? Maybe a shopping mall? Maybe a resort in some exotic country so I can have a drink as I watch my own despair?

At this point, the only thing that's certain is the uncertainty. And if there's anything that people hate in life, it's precisely uncertainty. We want to be certain of every possible outcome in everything we do. Learning to be comfortable with the fact that we can't always predict everything and be correct a hundred percent of the time is much harder than it sounds.

I gulp down my nervousness, grasp the doorknob, and look beside me at Peri. He nods in approval, and I proceed to turn the knob. I open the door and set foot inside of its darkness. As Peri follows me in and closes the door behind him, I feel like I've entered the vastness of outer space and I'm floating away.

I pace around as the new setting is being constructed by the glimmer, which doesn't take too long this time around. I had assumed that with each passing door, the environments would grow larger but this new one seems like it's the smallest one yet. It's even smaller than Mr. Baker's guidance office. Once the glimmer stops moving and it fills the environment up with colour, I let out a smile.

For the first time, I recognize where we are before my memory has been restored to inform me. I know the movie posters on the wall, the pop culture bobbleheads on the display stands, the history books next to the DVDs on the shelves, the laptop on the desk, and the black curtains covering up the two windows. This place is none other than my old bedroom!

I can't help but feel overjoyed as I view all the things I had collected over the years. I used to point my finger at my parents for turning me into a movie fanatic. They always had some old-school classic playing on the television, with most of them being in black and white. I wasn't much of a materialistic person but I loved owning what few items I did, especially if they had anything to do with movies or history.

"Well, this is a pleasant surprise," I say.

Peri's casually examining all the various items displayed around my room as if it were a museum. He picks up one of the bobbleheads that's shaped like an alien and gives the plastic figure a tiny shake. "Interesting, but what's the point of these?"

"To be honest, not much. They just look cool and they're fun to collect because there's so many of them. Some people make it a hobby to pass the time," I say.

Peri gives it one more shake before gently placing it back on the display stand.

All four walls of the bedroom are covered in various posters I had collected over the years from movie theatres to sales from my college campus. The excitement that I have right now from seeing them is how I must've felt when I first bought them. With all this excitement, however, follows confusion.

"Are you sure this is what I'm supposed to be experiencing?" I ask. "I don't see what could possibly happen here. It's only my bedroom, nothing else."

"This is definitely the right place," Peri says.

As my eyes glaze across the wall, I view a picture of Annie sitting on her hospital bed with me. A poignant smile forms on my face. She was so sweet, innocent, and kind. If only she was able to leave the hospital one time after I met her. I would've shown her all my collectibles and played my favourite movies for her, which she would've immensely enjoyed.

I walk over to one of the windows and look outside. It appears to be late at night and there's snow gently falling to the ground. There are two cars parked in the driveway and I analyze the rest of the street stretching down beyond my house. There's no one outside as if it's a ghost town. To get a better sense of the day and time, I view a mini calendar displayed on the laptop screen as its lid is open on the desk.

Saturday, January 20. 5:42 p.m.

I'm thinking as hard I can, but I have no clue about what could've happened on an ordinary January afternoon in my bedroom. I notice a document file that's minimized on the laptop screen at the bottom. I click and open it to see if it may provide any clues. It seems to be a poem.

Do you know what it feels like when your mind is in a dark place?
You were competing against life but ended up losing the race
You were once on top of the world and felt like a superhero
Then you came crashing down and ended up at ground zero
Your favourite sit-com is no longer funny
You don't have the drive to work and earn money
You don't feel the need to go out and socialize
You're a prisoner in your own home but people don't realize
This sickness of the mind hits you hard like a storm
You question your purpose and ask why you were born
It's an invisible force that can affect you at any time
You're suffering on the inside but you tell people you're fine
It doesn't matter if you're poor or rich, living off welfare or fame
No one is exempt, rest in peace Avicii, Kate Spade, and Anthony Bourdain

You used to laugh out loud but now you can't even crack a smile
Wishing you could return to childhood and relive that carefree lifestyle
Food begins to taste bland and the grass isn't as green
You're isolated and alone, not part of a team
You check your social media to view others' happiness and you feel envious
The further you scroll down, the more your thoughts become venomous
You feel like no one really cares about you, so you won't care about them
Nothing can help you, not even a vacation, a workout, or a bottle of rum
You can't recall when this feeling started or why it started
Your body's still functioning but your soul has departed
Maybe your partner left you, a friend used you, or a family member let you down
Like a lifeguard watching you struggle in the water and letting you drown
Now you're stranded in the blackness and silence of outer space
This is what it feels like when your mind is in a dark place

As soon as I've finished reading the last word, the emotional floodgate within my mind opens and many of my memories come rushing back to me like overwhelming rapids. I lose my balance and take a seat on the bed right next to the desk.

The trigger has been pulled without my past self even being present here. For some reason, I'm able to feel what he's feeling because he must be close by. This may be the longest jump in time yet, as I begin remembering everything over the course of years.

The emotions I feel the most right now are pain and suffering. My mind feels as cold, dark, and desolate as the street outside of my house in the dead of winter.

"Breathe a little, you've tensed up," Peri says. "What are you thinking about?"

"This is a long time after I graduated from college," I say. "I think this is four years later, so I should be 26 here. I was still living at home with my parents at the time and I felt like I hadn't made any progress in my life."

That's the vanilla version of it. My heart feels exceedingly heavy and my mind feels numb. All the joy and excitement I was experiencing from seeing my old belongings in my room has instantly evaporated.

I'm recalling nothing but dark and depressing thoughts from that specific time in my life. That poem that I'd once written on my laptop encompasses the precise state of mind that I was enduring. The pessimistic thoughts that my past self is feeling attack me from every direction. It's a jumbled mess of random issues that once made me very unhappy and extremely unmotivated to do anything.

It's such a cold winter this year...
The days aren't getting any brighter... I hate that it gets dark so early...
Why couldn't my parents have moved somewhere with more sunshine like California?
I must have that thing call seasonal affective disorder or something...

I'm tired… I have no energy…
There's nothing to look forward to anymore…
Why am I still living at home with my parents?
There's nothing to show for my progress besides a useless degree…
I'm not making or saving enough money…
What is our purpose in this universe?
I haven't left my house in days now…
I shouldn't have stopped exercising…
I could use another drink…
I'm fine though…
I'm okay…

"These are some of the worst thoughts yet," I say to Peri. "I feel like giving up without anything actually happening to me. It's like some serious existential crisis."

"There are times in our lives when our spirit is simply broken," Peri says. There doesn't have to be an event attached to it or a specific reason behind it. Sometimes, we just feel down and want to give up."

I think about all the previous doors and how this one is so much more different. The first door was linked to my relationship with my dad, the second to my high school math class, the third to my former group of friends, and the fourth to my guilt from not saving Bella. This fifth door doesn't seem to be linked to anything at all besides me having a rainy day. To be more specific, it feels like several rainy weeks in a row without any hope for sunshine.

The bedroom door swings open and in walks my past self. I'm frozen like I've seen the same ghost for the fifth time now. The sensation of being able to view myself like this is always surreal, no matter how many times it happens.

Past Danny is wearing typical clothes for home, a white full-sleeved shirt with light grey sweatpants. He has a beard growing that looks like it hasn't been trimmed in weeks. There's a plate in his hands with a sandwich on it. He closes the door behind him and takes a few steps toward his desk before sitting down in his chair.

I remain sitting on the bed next to him and I watch his every move. As my past self eats his sandwich and edits his poem, I'm thinking about all the questions I would ask him if he could hear me.

If you had one chance to meet a younger version of yourself, what would you ask? What kind of advice would you provide? Would you point out anything specific to avoid? Would you say nothing at all and allow life to run its natural course or would you try to change something and alter your path?

"He... I looked completely normal here," I say.

"You do. Most people look normal as if nothing's wrong. But keep in mind that sometimes, the people who look the most 'normal' on the outside can be the most damaged on the inside," Peri says.

Gloomy and miserable thoughts continue to swirl around in my mind as I feel what my past self feels.

"I was in a really dark place here. I thought I was a failure, and I didn't know how to cope with it alone," I say.

As soon as I'm done talking, the bedroom door swings open again. To my surprise, it's the person that lights up my world and the person I needed to see now more than ever. It's my mom!

She appears much older than she was in the memory with me at the arcade. Her hair contains more grey strands within it and her face has more wrinkles, but she's still as lovely as ever. What I would give to be able to hug her right now after all I've seen and been through. She's the only person who would never turn her back on me no matter what.

"Hey Danny, how's the sandwich?" my mom asks.

"It's good," Past Danny replies. "Thanks for making it."

"No problem. Come downstairs later if you're free. We can watch a movie together?" my mom asks.

"Okay, I'll let you know," Past Danny says.

My thoughts indicate otherwise, as he's thinking about staying here in his room and sleeping early tonight.

"Is everything alright?" my mom asks.

"Yeah, I'm fine," Past Danny says with a fake smile to reassure her.

"Are you sure? You know you can talk to me about anything," she responds.

"I know, I'm just finishing up some work here. I'm okay, I swear," Past Danny says, knowing well enough that he isn't okay at all.

"If you say so Danny. Well, let me know if you need anything else," my mom says before she exits and gently closes the door.

Past Danny breathes in and lets out an audible sigh as he sits in silence. He continues to eat his sandwich while he edits his poem. Whatever he's thinking right now is simultaneously being imprinted in my mind. There are so many thoughts to filter out, but I narrow them down as best as I can.

I should've told my mom the truth. I'm not feeling well. I'm having a hard time cheering up. What am I supposed to do? I keep saying that I'm fine when I know I'm not. I'm depressed.

This last thought hits me hard. At this point in my life, I had admitted the fact that I was suffering from depression. Despite all my pleasant experiences since I graduated from college, like visiting the children's hospital, there was something off about me in the years that passed. I didn't feel like the same person that I once was, and I wasn't sure how to address this change within me.

I was completely fine on some days but on others, I underwent a dreadful phase where my dark thoughts wouldn't leave me alone in peace. I eventually realized that I wasn't experiencing temporary mood swings, but that there was something more severe transpiring within my mind.

I had always downplayed this awful feeling and I tried to run away from it my whole life. When I finally stopped running, I acknowledged my mind was eating itself up from all the pessimism attached to it. It was constantly thinking about all the negative memories since my childhood and there was no way for me to ignore them.

I kept my depression a secret from everyone around me and I didn't even hint at its possibility. One of my greatest concerns was someone else telling me that I have so much to be grateful for and because of that, I shouldn't have any reasons to feel down in my life. The last thing that my ears wanted to hear was that there are millions of people around the world who are starving, let alone in a position to enjoy an entire bedroom to themselves. Why should I have any reason to be depressed?

I didn't want anyone comparing my individual suffering to others who are less fortunate than me. I also didn't want anyone lecturing me about how my problems are totally insignificant next to other people's problems from different neighborhoods, countries, or continents.

It's not that I didn't feel any sympathy for the less fortunate or that I didn't appreciate what I had. My heart bleeds for people who can't enjoy the necessities of life, like little kids who can't get an education. I've always been as thankful as I could be for all my blessings.

With that said, suffering is relative to an individual's unique situation in life. No one can genuinely understand that pain except for that individual alone. A wealthy billionaire who owns twenty properties, drives ten cars, and eats more than five nutritious meals a day can still be depressed to the point of taking their own life. On the other hand, an impoverished labourer who lives on rent, has to use public transportation, and eats only once a day can somehow find more happiness, comfort, and meaning in their existence. Maybe that person has more social support or maybe they simply have a more positive outlook and stay hopeful for better days to come. Either way, it's all about perspective, which is what most people seem to miss or don't understand about depression.

While I didn't think that my own mom would criticize or compare me to anyone, I still didn't want to take the chance to open myself up to her. I thought that if I did, my words may seem too much like a desperate cry for help or that I was seeking some attention with my vulnerability. I also didn't want my mom to worry about any of my personal problems because I felt that they were solely my burden to carry. I was being tormented on the inside and I would keep it that way before anyone else found out about it.

"I wouldn't wish a feeling like this on anyone, not even my worst enemies," I say to Peri. "It's a real sickness of the mind."

"You've been through some tough times, there's no doubt about it," Peri replies.

"The worst part about this feeling is how unpredictable it is. When it randomly comes and goes like a storm. When you can't even figure out why it's happening to you in the first place," I say.

Past Danny stops editing the poem and saves his work before closing the lid of his laptop. He stands up from his chair and then crouches down next to his bed, searching for something beneath the frame. He slides out a bottle of rum that appears to be half empty.

Great... This is about to add a whole new layer of crazy thoughts. I remember this bottle was one of many. I had developed a slight addiction to alcohol because I considered it to be the ultimate solution for my internal issues. The truth was that it only ever made them worse. Alcohol may temporarily help you escape your harsh reality, but you still have to face that reality after regardless. All it really does is merely delay the inevitable.

"Drinking won't help you," I say out loud to my past self, knowing that he can't hear a single word.

Past Danny twists the cap off the rum bottle and pours a large amount in one of the empty cups on his desk.

"Stop being an idiot," I urge him, as my advice falls on deaf ears.

I lean in to investigate his cup and see how much liquid he poured in there. This is the type of drink that surely makes a person lose their sensitivity to the rest of the world.

"Please... Don't be like dad," I continue.

Past Danny sits down in his chair, ready to drink his demons away for the time being. I stay seated on top of the bed right next to him. With one last attempt, I despairingly try to take the cup away from him and my hand goes right through it. I admit defeat and give up, like how Past Danny has given up on everything.

I sit anxiously on the bed next to him, knowing that any further words and actions are meaningless here. Past Danny takes a few sips of his drink and then proceeds to pull out his cellphone from his pocket.

Something strange begins to happen to me, as if things aren't strange enough already. I feel a burning sensation trickling down my throat to my stomach. I glance over at Peri, who's standing at the other side of the room and observing what's going on. My body begins to feel warm while my mind starts to loosen its tight grip.

Past Danny slumps down in his chair and gets comfortable before consuming more of his drink. If there weren't enough thoughts racing around in my mind, they've been amplified to the next level now. It's evident that with each gulp of rum that Past Danny drinks, I'm somehow feeling the same effects of it on my own mind.

So, I somehow ended up in a forest, then I walked through a magical door that led me to my old bedroom, and now I'm experiencing my past self get drunk. This almost feels like a dream within a dream... within another dream. My mind is starting to become one huge mishmash of information. My current thoughts and memories are being blended with Past Danny's erratic drunken thoughts.

Past Danny chugs down the rest of his drink and lets out a brief sigh. As the last drop travels down his throat, I slouch back on the bed next to him. I close my eyes and try to decipher my past self's tipsy thoughts as best as I can.

What did I do to deserve this? I've never hurt anyone. I've always been truthful, hard-working, and kind. Why is it that good people suffer while horrible people continue to thrive?

Are all these thoughts from my past self or are some of them mine from right now? My mind has become a gigantic cluster of random ideas, opinions, criticisms, beliefs, and ambiguous statements. I can't do anything now but to sit back and let them flow freely.

Now I know why my dad drank so much. I didn't get it as a child but I'm beginning to understand what he may have been going through. That doesn't mean I forgive him… it just means I can relate to him. But then again, why did he have to treat me so horribly? What did I ever do to annoy him so much? I tried my best to be a good son. I guess it is what it is. Everyone's dealt different cards in life.

There's a pain in my heart that's not easily extinguishable. It's difficult to openly criticize one of your parents who was supposed to be your greatest role model in life. My dad had single-handedly twisted my childhood into a life of fear and tension from his impulsiveness. As I became older, my dad gradually reduced his insulting behaviour toward me because he knew I wasn't so small and weak anymore. That didn't help as much as I thought it would because my internal scars never fully healed.

I remember feeling a whole range of confusing emotions toward my dad throughout my adult years. Anger, sadness, sympathy, regret, and disappointment to name a few. While my mom was always there for me, my dad was pretty much absent in all regards. He had a major impact on my mental health for all the wrong reasons. While I don't think that I could ever truly hate my dad, I most definitely can never love him.

Why am I always thinking about dad when I drink? What a waste of time. Let's see what people are up to on social media. Or in other words, media that isn't really social. A bunch of people liking and sharing worthless pictures that have absolutely no effect on their life whatsoever… But let's take a look anyway.

Was I really this bitter toward everyone else? My eyes remain shut as I try to figure out what could've possibly gotten me in or out of this depressed mindset.

Unfunny memes… Shameless advertising… Some radical nonsense… Meaningless posts… I really don't care about a picture of your lunch and a glass of wine that you're holding out on a patio… Congratulations, but what is the point of any of this? Is this all there is to life nowadays?

My mind is spinning as if it's been hypnotized, not only from the alcohol but from Past Danny's drifting through the rabbit hole of social media. Each time he scrolls through his feed, new posts arrive to indulge in. It's no different than a slot machine at a casino. Instead of pulling a mechanical lever down, you swipe upward and hope for a new result each time. Both are games of chance where you end up feeling more disappointed than satisfied.

Someone posted about a wedding reception that's going to have over a thousand guests... Are you trying to win a gold medal in the Pretentious Show-Off Games? Is there nothing authentic or humble on social media? I keep telling myself I'm going to deactivate my account, but I end up hanging on to it out of curiosity. I don't want to feel like I'm missing out on anything.

I'll never forget the very first time I made a social media account and what my initial reaction was. I was in early middle school at the time, so I lied about my age to sneak past the minimum limit and sign up. I was excited to enter this totally new world of communication, but my high expectations were far from the reality that followed.

I felt nothing but confusion when I scratched my itch to use social media for the first time. I remember thinking, why would people want to post personal status updates or write on each other's walls when they could easily talk to each other in person? Fast forward many years later and social media became the new standard of communication around the world.

There are a lot of good things to be found on social media but over time, I realized that the negative aspects far outweigh them. To name a few, the constant comparisons to other people's happiness, the time that's wasted from lack of productivity, and the observance of strangers' lifestyles while lamenting your own. Everyone's racing in their own lane but when you're more focused on them instead of keeping your eyes on the track in front of you, it becomes easy to lose sight of all the progress you've made.

When you constantly see other people boasting about the job they're working, where they're going for vacation, or when they're getting married, you start to question and criticize your own situation more often than you should. Deep down, you know that these milestones aren't necessary to achieve in order to live a good life, but you often forget that. You begin pondering about why you're slower than the rest of the crowd and why you're struggling to keep up with them. No one ever wants to feel left behind. The endless overexposure to other others' posts on social media can be a recipe for disaster and be responsible for creating envy, one of the most perilous emotions in existence.

More arguments over political issues... All these people wasting their energy on writing toxic paragraphs aimed at others who disagree with their views. When are people going to realize that you can never win an online argument? Trying to have a debate with someone on the internet is like talking to a brick wall to tear it down. You can fling as many comments as you want at it, but it won't budge and make a difference.

In all the many years since social media has become the staple of our society, I've yet to see just one person concede to another in an argument online. It's as if it's impossible for someone to admit defeat and comment, "Hey you know what? You made some great points against me! I agree with you. Have a nice day!" Unfortunately, the real world isn't as open-minded, respectable, or generous like that.

Wow, what a great selfie! I'm having a blast looking at your edited and filtered face... Next... Cool, what an amazing body! Let us know how many steroids it took for you to look that way! Next... More unrealistic beauty standards. How absurd is this? What does the younger crowd think about this stuff? Where do we draw the line?

I sound extremely annoyed in my mind, but then I begin thinking about all the young kids and teenagers out there who are growing up in a world in which scrolling through social media is their daily source of entertainment. The days are long gone when kids like me were trying to fill that same quota by watching their favourite cartoons on a Saturday morning.

From the minute they wake up to the minute they fall asleep, how many times do today's kids view some online content that makes them feel lost or bad about themselves? How many models, actors, athletes, content creators and other celebrities have influenced teenagers in some way, with their "perfect" facial features, make-up routines, and altered bodies? How often do those comparisons make them feel like rubbish and play a key role in taking away their self-esteem? If there's anything I've noticed, it's that social media contributes to declining mental health and depression more than it helps alleviate it.

Past Danny's thoughts are relentless as he continues to scroll down his never-ending social media feed like a mindless zombie. Post after post, his scrolling becomes faster and faster. I can sense his frustration building up by the second.

Food posts… More selfies… Sports highlights… Garbage music clips… Cringe videos… I guess this is supposed to be the latest viral dance… Simply life-changing stuff.

Past Danny then comes across a post that makes him freeze up. He remains on it longer than any previous post and his initial reaction isn't as hostile toward it. It's a picture of his friends, Sylvia and James.

I hope you guys are doing alright in medical school. It wouldn't hurt you to message me once in a while but it's all good. You guys are busy with your studies… and with each other. I don't even know if we're still friends anymore but maybe we'll try hanging out when you're back home.

I remember that Sylvia and James had left the country to go to America and pursue their medical degree, while I remained at home with my arts degree. Initially, we did keep in touch but as time went on, our communication declined to the point where we didn't talk for months.

It didn't help that they ended up in a relationship and spent most of their time together. I felt like I went from being one of the three musketeers to suddenly becoming the unwanted third wheel.

How many groups of friends have I chased in my life, only to be thrown to the curb without any appreciation? Far too many... Or maybe the problem has always been with me because I suck at keeping in touch with everyone... Truthfully, I don't know what it is. I think I've become desensitized to friendships now with no interest in pursuing new ones. There's more to lose than there is to gain.

This last post with Sylvia and James seems to have sparked the most interest as it's generating the most discussion within my mind.

Why couldn't they message me here and there? I guess I could've messaged them as well. Now it feels like it's too late so I'm not going to bother... It would be all small talk anyway... But then again, what's the point of owning a smartphone if you can't even use it to keep in touch with someone close to you? I don't know.

You feel the greatest impact from a lack of communication when it's related to the people who are closest to you. I could've swallowed my pride and messaged Sylvia or James, two of my closest friends. I'm trying to process how any of this makes sense and how everyone ended up here in the first place.

Smartphones and social media made it so much easier to communicate with others around the globe, more than ever before in human history, yet we're more isolated and further apart. Somehow, we're more emotionally disconnected within this technologically connected world we're living in.

I recall the waning days when people used to be genuinely thrilled about receiving messages because they had to build anticipation for them. It may seem inconvenient now but the old saying went, *good things come to those who wait.*

I remember the days when people still received hand-written letters in the mail and they eagerly read their long-awaited replies, before any lightning-quick emails and text messages would constantly bombard them. The days when people still received occasional phone calls from their relatives halfway around the world, before any smartphones and data plans would replace their lengthy conversations with convenience. The days when people still developed their photos and carefully inserted them into their cherished albums, before any tiny cameras in their pockets would store thousands of soulless snapshots.

It's not that I despise technology, but everything before it seemed to have more meaning, love, and enthusiasm attached with it. Nowadays, it feels like that's no longer present. The frequent notifications we receive on a daily basis have become synonymous with mundane chores we must complete. The online interactions we have with others can sometimes be no different than communicating with a robot without any emotion. The infinite photos that we take and the videos that we record are scarcely revisited in the years to come.

That'ssss enuff for won knight… I think eye reallyyy knead to deleep my focal meadia… thyme to shleep now…

At last, I open my eyes as Past Danny is too far gone and drunk. He's slumped in his chair with the alcohol coursing through his veins and both eyes struggling to remain open. The final post he views before exiting his social media is a video of someone lifting weights.

Peri is leaned up against the wall with both of his arms crossed. "That took a while. Are you alright?"

"No," I reply. "I'm feeling so much negativity and animosity toward everyone. Everything's making me feel sad and angry. From the depressing weather to the dark winter days, my supposed friends not staying in touch, my alcohol addiction, my tiredness, my contempt for social media, lack of a solid job, my living situation, and questioning my very purpose on this planet. I was 26 at the time and I had nothing to show for it. I felt like I couldn't catch a break."

"I can sense your discomfort and pain. You were at rock bottom here and no one else knew about it, not even your mom," Peri says.

"Writing in my spare time was the only thing that helped me express what I was going through," I say.

"Well, something is better than nothing," Peri says. "All of us fight our own battles on the inside. For some of us, the battle is to simply survive the day and hopefully see a new one tomorrow. We have to keep hoping for better days ahead Danny."

"I don't want to say this, but there were days when I contemplated taking my own life. That's how hopeless I was at this point," I admit.

"Trust me, that's never the solution," Peri says. "There's so much to experience in the world. It can be tough to replace misery with happiness, but it's possible if you put your mind to it."

"I'll need to see it to believe it after this experience," I say.

"Let us move on then. To a better time when you managed to overcome this negative thinking," Peri says.

I get up from the bed and take one last look at Past Danny. His eyelids are closed shut and he's fallen asleep in his chair. Even though he can't physically feel me, I place my right hand on my past self's shoulder.

I want to tell him that I know what he's going through and he's not alone. I wasn't only slumped in my chair here, but I was also slumped in my life. I can feel him trying to fight the raging battle within his mind as he sleeps. It's a battle between the emerging light against the darkness that's taken hold of him.

I nod my head at Peri to let him know I'm ready to leave. I look around the room and take in the sight one last time before our departure. I view the DVD collection behind the assorted bobbleheads. All these material items that once provided me with so much joy have become relics of a bygone era. Perhaps one day, they'll mean something to me again. Until then, farewell old bedroom.

Peri raises his hand and snaps his fingers, causing everything to instantly fade away like dust being blown into the wind. It becomes dark all around us for a few moments.

I recall sitting in a theatre with my mom as a kid. I didn't mind being in the dark then because we were so excited to watch a movie together. I keep wondering where she could be now and if she's alright. I hope to be finished with this crazy night soon because she'll be the first person I visit as soon as I'm out of here.

The glimmer begins to create the new environment around me and Peri. What could've taken me out of this destructive state of mind? I felt like I had no strength or confidence to grow and develop myself. I was performing poorly in all aspects of my life: mentally, physically, financially, and spiritually.

The glimmer outlines various items and expands the stage into an area larger than my bedroom. Whenever the setting shifts from one place to another, it's as if we're changing sets on a Broadway performance with rotating actors.

As the glimmer completes the transition and fills the new scene with colour, I recognize where we're standing once again. The objects laid out in front of me are very specific and distinguishable from other environments. I see an abundance of free weights, benches, treadmills, ellipticals, stationary bicycles, machines, medicine balls, and yoga mats. We're standing in the middle of a gym that I used to exercise in.

I walk over to a large mirror that covers an entire wall behind a rack of weights. I'm unable to view my physical reflection but I recall doing so in my younger years. I tread around the area and examine this familiar place that I must now be a part of for the next while. The dials on one of the analog clocks on the wall displays 11:30. This memory is occurring some time in the morning then, as it's a bright and clear day outside from the windows.

I anxiously await my past self to show up and anticipate more of my memories to be restored to my mind. Hopefully, they act like a spoon of medicine after how drained I've become since my bedroom. If there's anything that these opposing positive memories do, it's that they make me feel a million times better about myself. They provide reassurance that the worst is behind me, which I need right now more than ever.

There are a few other people present in this gym, exercising around me and Peri. The weights are clanking and the treadmills are whirring.

"Are you trying to get a workout in right now?" Peri teases.

"You already know," I say, trying not to sound too serious.

Peri suddenly drops down to the ground and starts doing push-ups in front of me. He starts out with a few but then to my surprise, goes past fifteen.

"Huh? How are you doing that many?" I ask, as Peri's not stopping or getting tired.

"I guess I'm super strong," Peri says while he continues to move up and down on the ground.

"Hold on a minute old man, we don't have any weight!" I say after realizing we're a pair of ghosts.

I drop down on the spot and start doing push-ups next to Peri. We do about forty each before calling it quits and we proudly get up like we've just competed at the Olympics.

"That was really hard," Peri says.

I smile as Peri pretends to wipe sweat off his forehead.

Despite this little bit of fun, I'm still feeling down inside knowing that my past self is on his own with no one helping him out. If only I had a solid friend or a mentor figure like Peri, who I could open myself up to whenever I was going through a depressed phase. If I had felt more comfortable talking about my issues with the right person, I know that it would've made a world of difference. I would've been able to release the dark demons caged inside of me that were tearing my soul apart day by day.

As I'm thinking about all the opportunities that I could've taken to improve my mental health, a bulky figure brushes right past me and Peri.

He's wearing dark grey running shoes, black shorts, and one of those long-sleeved white gym shirts that outlines his muscular upper body. He casually walks over to the weights section and starts stretching. Judging from his back, I assume he's one of those massive bodybuilders that practically live in the gym.

A small detail catches my eye. There's something familiar about his headphones. They're a distinctive red colour. I glance over at Peri before I take a few steps forward toward the area with the weights. I approach this figure and slowly circle around him, about to confirm or deny who he is. Once I'm close enough, my mouth is agape.

"Wait… This can't be me," I say to myself.

I move in even closer and we're now standing face-to-face. My dark brown eyes are being reflected right back at me and my short stubble beard is back. This is my face, but the rest of my body has undergone a serious transformation.

I looked nothing close to this in my bedroom, as I recall last seeing myself drunk, weak, and passed out in my chair. Past Danny's legs are now toned, his chest is bulging, his biceps and triceps are made of steel, his shoulders are the size of boulders, and his back looks like it could carry a mountain. He looks like a beast with significantly more muscle mass, which is almost intimidating to a certain degree.

Past Danny drops down to do some push-ups as Peri and I watch his performance. As he breezes past thirty push-ups without breaking a sweat, I blankly stare at him. My mind is debating if this is even the same person who was in my bedroom.

"Are you sure this isn't some crazy evil twin of mine?" I ask Peri.

"Oh, it's you alright… and you just did more push-ups than we did," Peri replies.

I lose count of how many push-ups my past self completed. He finally gets up and looks pumped up like I've never seen before. He performs some more stretches before approaching the rack that holds a selection of weights. Past Danny then picks up a pair of sixty-pound dumbbells and finds an incline bench to settle down in. He adjusts his position to get comfortable and waits a few seconds with a weight sitting on each thigh. It's like a rocket preparing to launch to outer space.

Once he's in the zone, Past Danny's rock-solid arms pick up the heavy weights and thrust them upward toward the moon. As soon as this action is performed, the trigger has been pulled and my former memories begin to hit my mind at once.

I begin to experience a warm sensation running throughout my entire body. It reminds me of the bottle of alcohol from my bedroom but instead of feeling groggy and slow, I feel so much healthier and more powerful. It appears that Past Danny has swapped out his liquor bottle for a protein shake bottle instead.

With the many memories that've been restored to my mind, I feel immensely relieved as I experience the same emotions as my past self. The strength, confidence, and certainty being built within this gym is a far cry from the weakness, vulnerability, and futility my mind was enduring in my bedroom. With each physical contraction that Past Danny performs using his weights, my mental state is undergoing an enlightenment. I express myself with a huge smile within this state of pure bliss.

With more of my former memories regained, I try to remember what happened after I had hit rock bottom and how I ended up here as a brand-new person.

This memory is taking place a few months after I was completely fed up with my life. I was wasting away my days boxed up inside of my bedroom without any inspiration to do anything. I had no direction and no purpose for what felt like an eternity. I thought I had considered all the possible solutions for this ongoing problem within me. From seeing a therapist to packing my bags and traveling somewhere far, I thought of many different options to try to fix myself.

One of those options made me realize that the most convenient remedy was right in front of me the entire time. It was much cheaper than any therapist and much closer to home than any remote destination. There was a night when I happened to stumble upon a short workout video online and instead of skipping over it, I began to watch it until its end. Soon after, the online algorithms worked their magic and began recommending more fitness-related videos for me to watch.

I knew that if my life continued the way that it was going, I'd end up in an early grave sooner or later. Because of my inability to reach out to other people, I knew that the only person who could truly save me from my own annihilation was myself. I had to force my mind to slap itself awake from all its cynicism first, so I rose to the challenge to prove that I could make some serious changes in my lifestyle.

I knew that the gym was a place that could help me accomplish this. It was a place where I could vent all my frustrations in while simultaneously making gains for my body and mind. In other words, it was a win-win situation that could potentially bring me out of my constant despair. It was time to commit myself and move on up because I couldn't sink any further down.

I first started exercising in high school to complement other sports I was playing. I participated in everything from soccer to basketball, volleyball, and running. In a way, the gym became a temple for me where I'd go worship by lifting weights and grow myself as a person by practising discipline. Even throughout my college days, I always managed to sneak in some exercise time into my schedule, whether it was in between lectures or during lunch.

The gym had been a special place for me but once I graduated from college, it slowly became neglected. As my intrusive depression became more frequent, any motivation and discipline I once had easily broke apart. Whenever I had one of those major setbacks, I would often think to myself, *what's the point?* Looking back at it now, this was the worst possible question to contemplate. That mentality was responsible for taking away all my hard work, determination, and progress that I was once so proud to achieve.

As I view Past Danny lifting a barbell for his bench press, I feel that same sense of pride within me again. It's not strictly about the physicality but more so the inherent drive and commitment to do better by taking care of myself. A few moments ago, I saw myself stuck inside of my bedroom like a jail, rum flowing throughout my body, childishly complaining about anything and everything. Now I'm watching myself lift heavy weights in this gym, pushing my mind and my body to its absolute limits with renewed vitality and focus. The difference is as good as night and day.

Peri taps me on the shoulder behind me. "How's it going muscle man?" he asks.

"This feels incredible… like I'm Superman. I feel like I'm on another level right now. It's like I've been cured!" I reply.

"If there's anything that this memory proves, it's that you have what it takes to overcome the struggles within you," Peri says. "Don't ever forget that."

I nod in agreement as other thoughts begin to cross my mind.

I think about all the people out there in the world who may have once excelled in something but abandoned it when they suffered through hard times.

What's the point?

It's one of the shortest questions we can ask ourselves, but also one of the most detrimental for our ambitions. How many interests, hobbies, unique talents, aspiring dreams, and remarkable abilities have been crushed under the weight of depression? How many musicians, athletes, artists, comedians, designers, and photographers have given up their craft because their mind began thinking it was meaningless and that they shouldn't pursue it anymore? Those very commitments that people shelve or eliminate entirely from their lives could have easily been their personal version of a "cure."

For me, this cure had always been exercising without me even knowing it. I didn't realize how much I needed the energy from running and pushing weights until I resumed it here after an exceedingly long break.

I remember feeling triumphant over my troubles by nurturing a positive mindset and by implementing many other subtle changes as well. From reading more books and limiting my social media time, to sending out more resumes and receiving job offers, to choosing protein shakes and nutritious meals over alcohol and junk food.

Although I may not have gone from poor to rich in terms of my finances, I became wealthy beyond measure from taking care of my body and mind. I remember changing the concept of mental health to mental *wealth* so that I could measure it from another perspective and emphasize its significance as a currency instead.

Most people assume that wealth can only be correlated with how much money is sitting in your checking or savings account. What they often fail to realize is that anyone can be rich financially but penniless physically, mentally, spiritually, intellectually, and socially. What good is being rich if you can't even stand on your own two legs because you've mistreated your body your whole life? Or what about if you're constantly insecure, can't find any inner peace, don't educate yourself about the world you live in, and have no one close to you?

Dollar bills won't seem nearly as important under those circumstances. By making a few small changes within your lifestyle, you can balance out these several "currencies" and revitalize your mindset. From that moment onward, being wealthy will encompass a completely different definition than the one you've been accustomed to learning since childhood.

Past Danny is on the pull-up bar now, working away while I rejoice in my positive thoughts. He's not only pulling his body up but the weight of the world along with him. It's an exhilarating sensation knowing how much of a difference a focused workout can make. All it takes is forcing yourself to uncover your hidden potential, especially when there may be no one else around to encourage you. As cheesy as it sounds, you truly do miss a hundred percent of the shots that you don't take. I must've heard that statement countless times since I was a little boy, but it hadn't rung truer until now.

"Relying on other people isn't always a sound strategy. It can be hard for them to motivate the unmotivated. But once you understand that you have the power to accomplish anything deep within you, there's nothing out there that can stop you. No matter what stands in your way," Peri says.

"I was definitely motivated here… and I did it all by myself. I feel pumped up, like I'm ready to go fight in a war," I say.

"Well, you *are* fighting a war. It's just not an obvious one," Peri says. "The previous memory with you in your bedroom was an example of you losing a battle in your mind. While you may lose a few battles along the way, it's never too late to win the war."

"You probably think I'm messed up from everything we've seen so far but I'm learning something new from each of these doors and memories. Thank you," I say.

"That's not true Danny, not at all. And don't thank me yet, we still have two more doors to get through," Peri says.

Past Danny stops exercising to take a rest break. It seems that he's forgotten his water bottle inside of the changing room, so he begins to walk out of the weights section. His confident stride doesn't break for a second and his continuous positive thoughts have me feeling reinvigorated.

I look down to view my own ghostly body. I'm not as bulky as my past self here but I still have a fair bit of muscle on me, which makes me believe that I didn't completely abandon the gym after this period in my life. I must've stuck with what I started, and that alone is an achievement for me.

Past Danny enters one of the changing room doors and as it closes behind him, a bright white light instantly shines from underneath it. There's our exit out of here, like all the previous doors.

"Another memory down Danny. You've seen how strong you can become, especially from within. Don't forget that your setbacks are only ever temporary," Peri says. "We can move on now if you're ready."

I take a final look at this environment that I didn't know would bring me so much optimism and satisfaction. If something as small as a gym could help me this much, then I'm sure it could help anyone. Spending a few minutes of your day on your physical and mental wellbeing can afford you a lifetime of fulfilment. All it takes is one strong initial push to get yourself started and the rest will continue naturally.

"Yeah, I'm ready Peri," I say.

I approach the same changing room door that my past self stepped into. There's no doorknob or handle on this heavier and bigger door, as it only requires a simple push forward. I see the white light protruding through the tiny slit at the bottom.

I push the door and I'm greeted by the shining light that beckons me to enter it. I take a few steps inside and Peri follows, ending another chapter in this mystifying journey. The sights and sounds of the gym fade away as the door closes behind us. The benches and the machines vanish while the whirring of the treadmills and the clanking of the weights fade into silence. I'm blinded by the euphoric light that makes me feel warm and comfortable. I only have two more doors left. I'm almost at the finish line now. I know I can do this.

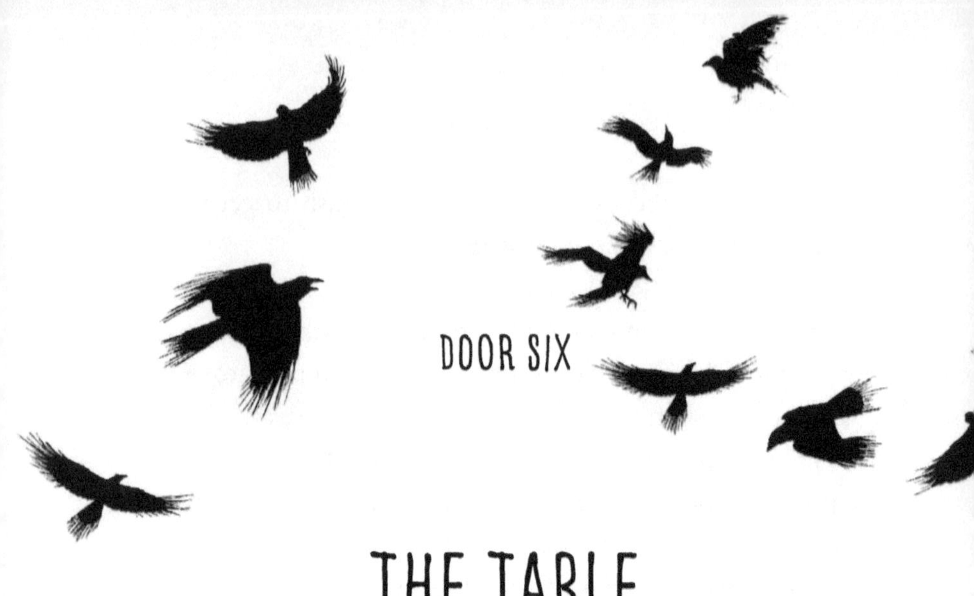

DOOR SIX

THE TABLE

The bright light fades away and I awaken on the ground. Peri outstretches his hand and helps me pick myself up. I confirm that the door we visited has vanished as the final two doors are left in front of me. I have no idea about what lays ahead. I've been through many painful experiences so far and I don't know how much worse it could get.

The fog has moved much closer since we've been gone. It's reached up to the point where the second door previously stood, making this clearing feel even more claustrophobic. The crows are flying around above the fog, close enough to encircle my head in the night sky. They're croaking as if they're speaking to me and warning me to hurry up.

"You've done well Danny," Peri says. "Many others usually give up by now and fail their trials."

Peri really is an unusual figure. Whenever I bombard him with questions, he responds in riddles or not at all. When I don't ask him anything, he reveals information that changes everything.

"Wait, others have been here before me? How? When?" I ask as I look around for any signs of life.

"Not exactly," Peri replies. "They go through their own tailored version of a dark forest and memory doors. Some people have more doors, some have less. Some make it to the end, while others are consumed by the fog if their will to survive isn't strong enough."

"Do you help them like you're helping me or does somebody else? How many people like you are out there?" I ask.

"It's only me who serves my master, no one else. I can't save everyone though. I can help the ones that have a higher chance of completing their trial, but there's still no guarantee that they will."

I'm scratching my head as Peri continues with his explanation.

"I'm able to take on many forms and I can be in many places at once, all around the world. My current form is what makes you feel most comfortable," Peri says.

"Ah yes, a senior who looks like he can pose no harm to me. Much better than an alpha male in a military uniform I suppose!" I reply. I'd be surprised to find something that actually obeys the laws of physics out here. "The fog isn't slowing down at all… What'll really happen to me if it gets close enough?"

"There won't be any way to escape it then. The window to return to your normal life will be closed forever," Peri replies. "There's still enough time to avoid that from happening, but not much. Let's keep this discussion short and move Danny."

I don't know what I may have done or said to deserve any of what's going on, but I accept my fate as my urgency to progress quickly returns. The darkness, fog, and crows are ready to devour my soul, but I'll keep them at bay for a little while longer. I nod my head at Peri in agreement and we walk toward the sixth door.

I've regained most of my memory but there's still few more pieces missing. I know what I must do to acquire the rest of them, but the worst may be yet to come. I recall the saying, *hope for the best and prepare for the worst.* It's not so easy doing either one, especially when the bad times in your life catch you off guard and break you down into pieces. Building an optimistic approach in life is difficult when your foundation isn't as strong as it should be.

"After completing these last two doors, I can return home?" I ask.

"Yes, you'll have your entire memory back and you'll be able to leave this forest," Peri confirms.

"I'm ready then," I say.

We stand in front of the sixth door that has a glow around it. My hand grasps the doorknob and I take a deep breath.

I know that staying strong is the key but when the bad memories flood my mind, it's as if I lose a bit of my sanity in the process because of how difficult they are to handle. Whatever it takes to get me home I suppose.

I turn the knob, open the door, and view the pitch-black abyss in front of me. I turn my head to Peri and he nods at me. I don't think I would've made it this far without him. I most likely would've forfeited long ago out of despair from one of the negative memories.

I take a few steps forward as Peri closes the door behind us. I'm left standing in complete emptiness. A blank, dark canvas that's ready to be molded into any one of the millions of environments out there.

The magical glimmer arrives and begins to outline the new setting for us. It creates a perfect mold of specific structures, people, items, and other materials that makes me feel like I'm in an alternate universe.

Sturdy-looking tables are formed within an enclosed establishment, along with wooden chairs, delicate hanging lights above, and a long serving counter. Once everything has been created precisely the way it's supposed to, the glimmer fills itself with colour and the environment is officially brought to life.

Before I inspect anything at all, I'm absolutely delighted by the stimulating smell in this environment. The smell of coffee beans fills the air, which hits my nostrils like an addictive drug. The scent fits in perfectly with the rest of the brown-coloured, dimmed ambience found within this place. It appears to be a local coffee shop, which is the perfect size and doesn't feel too empty.

There are pleasing illustrations that are framed and hung up on the walls, along with an antique clock. There's a busy street that's visible from the windows beside the entrance. It's a gloomy day outside with rain pouring down and pedestrians trying to keep themselves dry with their umbrellas.

Peri takes a seat on one of the bar stools in front of the serving counter while looking up at the menu.

"What would you like?" he jokes.

"I'll take a bagel with butter and a medium coffee. Two cream and two sugar," I reply with a smile.

I haven't eaten or drank anything since I've been in the forest, but my stomach hasn't seemed to notice. It's alright, I'll have plenty of time for that once I'm free from here.

Either my past self is already sitting in this coffee shop somewhere or he'll be arriving shortly. I stroll around the place and stop at each table to analyze the people sitting in their chairs. Let's see who we have here.

A middle-aged woman with her baby eating lunch… Nope. Two elderly men with grey beards reading their newspapers and discussing politics… No again, at least not yet. Four teenagers sipping on their iced coffees and talking about sports… Maybe if I were younger but no for now. A man checking his text messages on his phone while facing the entrance… I need to get a better look at this candidate. He appears to be waiting for someone else as he hasn't ordered any food or drink yet.

As I swing around this figure, my eyes become locked in on his face. I've gotten used to the rhythm of identifying my past self with my facial features. More than anything else, it's the dark brown eyes that do the trick and help me detect myself the quickest. There's a certain look to them that's so familiar and engrained within my mind. Maybe it's from all the times I would blankly stare at myself in the mirror, questioning what I'm doing with my life.

After a few seconds of analyzing have concluded, I confirm that this man sitting by himself is me. He has the same secretive eyes as me, which have become an expert in hiding a world of pain behind them. Past Danny seems to look a few years older since the last time I saw him in the gym. He's wearing a nice outfit consisting of dark pants, dress shoes, and a burgundy sweater. His black coat is hung up behind his chair beside his umbrella. There's my stubble beard as well, which has developed into my signature style at this point.

I help myself to an empty chair right in front of him. I'm sitting face-to-face with a younger version of myself as if we're about to casually share what's new in our lives over a cup of coffee.

I notice that Past Danny is wearing the same vintage watch that I'm currently wearing. It's a bit less worn and torn than mine, but it has the same gleaming white face and a dark brown strap. Oddly enough, this one watch on my wrist has been there with me throughout most of my memories. It seems as if it's the one and only constant amid all the chaos and ambiguity.

I view the silver hands on its face that are slowly ticking away. I then look around this coffee shop and think about how everyone here is unknowingly getting older by the second. The young teenagers, the middle-aged woman with her toddler, as well as the elderly seniors.

I've always been mesmerized by the concept and perception of time. It's something that's been moving in a forward direction since the creation of the universe, something that we can't reverse no matter how hard we try. The past is the past and whatever happened has happened. Our present and future may be changeable, but we're still vulnerable in the face of our ultimate end.

The hands on the face of a watch endlessly travel in a clockwise direction, which is a false representation of our lives. As its time will continue ticking in circles long after we're gone from this world, it undoubtedly portrays an illusion. It makes us feel that the time we possess is not limited but instead, an everlasting loop.

I believe that an hourglass is more brutally honest and realistic in its depiction of the moments that pass us by. Those tiny grains of sand slowly drop down and accumulate at the bottom, representing the time that's gone and what we can't retrieve. The rest of the finite grains remain at the top, alerting us of how much fleeting time is left and leaving us with the important question of what to do with it.

It's strange how much a simple and trivial item can make you think about life, but I guess that's the beauty of it. Perhaps one day, I'll gift this watch to my future child and pass it down to the next generation. It'll be a small way to keep my insignificant memory alive. Something that's tangible, wearable, and more personal than a photograph of me could ever be.

I regain my composure and stop my thoughts from drifting any further. I focus my attention back on Past Danny sitting across from me, who's busy on his phone. I get up from my chair and lean in to see what he's scrolling through. It's a short text message from someone named Maya.

Be there at 4.

The antique clock on the wall near me displays 3:57 p.m., so whatever is happening is about to begin soon. I leave my chair and walk over to Peri who's lounging in the background, as he usually does when I experience these memories.

"So, my past self is waiting over there at that table for someone to eat lunch with… This memory doesn't seem to be anything major," I say.

"Oh, it's pretty major. Wait and see," Peri says.

Peri's acting like that one friend who's recently watched a new movie and doesn't want to spoil it so that you can enjoy it more. In this case, however, I'm pretty sure that I'm not about to enjoy what's to come.

The door at the entrance of the coffee shop swings open. A woman emerges from the dimness of the outside world with an umbrella in her hand. The rain is still pouring outside but she's managed to keep herself dry. She has black hair and spellbinding eyes that are a sight to behold. She's carrying a small purse by her side and wearing blue pants with a white top that has black stripes running across it.

Past Danny reacts to this woman's entrance by putting his phone away in his pocket. He stands up as she approaches his table. In the meantime, I sit in a chair at the table beside them, patiently waiting to see what transpires here.

"Hey Maya," Past Danny says. "How are you?"

"Fine," she replies.

They both sit down in their seats across from one another.

"You want to order? I heard these guys have great coffee and marble cake," Past Danny suggests.

"I don't want anything Danny," Maya says.

"Okay… So how have you been?" Past Danny asks.

"Can we skip the formalities and please get this over with?" Maya asks.

What's going on here? Either I must've really messed something up or this Maya lady is having a really bad day. I'm trying to form an idea of who she may be, but nothing comes to mind. My memory only extends as far as what I received from the last door, which was me in the gym at 26.

Wait a minute… I notice Maya's hands fidgeting beneath the table out of nervousness and tension. She's wearing a ring on her left hand, and it's not any ordinary ring. It's an engagement ring. There's no way… Could she be? I continue listening in on their conversation to pick up more clues.

"Come on Maya, relax. We're out here in public. Just act normal for once," Past Danny says.

"Don't tell me to relax. I didn't come here to have a nice lunch or whatever. I came here for closure," Maya says.

"Can we at least order coffee? There's people around, please don't make a scene now," Past Danny says.

"I don't care man. I told you I don't want anything from you," Maya snaps back. She has a fierce look in her eyes.

"Is that all you have to say? What will our families think about us?" Past Danny asks.

"I told you before, there is no more *us*," Maya says. Beneath the table, she rips the engagement ring off her finger and slams it down on the table in front of Past Danny.

As soon as that happens, the trigger has officially been pulled. I lower my head on the table in between my arms, as my memories scurry in and begin to cram my mind. I keep my head down and try to remember as much as I can to fill in the time gap.

This moment in the coffee shop is slightly over three years after the memories from my bedroom and gym in the previous door. I was 29 years old here and I had attained somewhat of a stable job as a history teacher in a private school. I thought that I was ready to embark on the next chapter of my life with marriage until it all fell apart.

I originally met Maya about a year before this moment, on a dating app of all places. It somehow became the norm in society with more accessible technology and declining in-person interactions.

I had always preferred the old-school method of physically approaching someone to strike up a conversation, but I decided to try online dating because of my busier work schedule. I should've known from that instant that there could be a major chance of us not working out, especially when it came down to a serious commitment. On the other hand, I had read a ton of stories about other people meeting their soulmates, best friends, and spouses online through various apps, so I thought why not?

The more Maya and I talked over the weeks after we first met, the more I became infatuated. I fell in love with the idea of someone else being out there in the world who was compatible with me and consistently on the same page as me.

As I'm consumed with my thoughts, a verbal argument is taking place in front of me between Past Danny and Maya. They're trying to keep it as passive aggressive as they can because they know they're not at home in private.

"You know, I could've ended things long ago when I first found those texts to your ex," Past Danny says. "I still gave you another chance after that."

"You had no right going through my phone in the first place. You were wrong for that," Maya replies.

"Oh, I was wrong? I wasn't the one texting any exes while in a relationship with you," Past Danny snaps back. He's starting to stray away from the calm state that he was in and he's beginning to divulge his angrier side.

With the memories and emotions fresh in my head, I recall that scene like it was yesterday.

I was renting a small place in Toronto while working at the private school, which was a massive step up for me because I moved out of my parents' home for the first time. Maya worked as a personal trainer and she would occasionally visit me, especially on Friday or Saturday evenings when we'd stay in and catch a movie together or go out to eat dinner.

I knew that she had broken up with her previous boyfriend a few weeks before meeting me, but I never thought much about it. Maya always reassured me that she found solace with me and that I was the best thing to have ever happened to her. One thing led to another, and I ended up asking her to be my girlfriend.

After a couple of months of joyful dating, there finally came a moment when our attitudes toward one another changed and were no longer aligned. One night while we were watching a movie at my place, Maya got up and went to the bathroom. She happened to leave her phone behind on the couch and it was unlocked. She *always* took it with her wherever she went, so this one time must've been a genuine mistake.

Before this, it had never even occurred to me that I would care about accessing her phone in any way. I trusted her as much as I could, and I was happy with her. In that moment, however, my mind briefly manipulated me and reminded me that trust can only go so far. I grew up trusting people like my abusive dad, my awful friends, and many others who were supposed to be there for me. I knew how those relationships turned out, so I was slightly skeptical even if I didn't want to be.

I saw Maya's phone laying there beside me and I thought about how this opportunity may never present itself again. My heart knew that it was wrong, but my mind instructed me otherwise. I had never been the snoopy type and it's not like I had any serious doubts about Maya, but my own curiosity ended up getting the best of me.

I decided to question Maya's trust for a few seconds as I proceeded to check her phone, clicking on the text messages app right away.

What I saw next was something that I truly wished I hadn't seen at all. That's when I found all the recently exchanged messages with her ex-boyfriend. Upon seeing them, the pain cut me so deep that it was unlike anything I had experienced before in my life.

His name was Zaire and while I knew Maya dated him for about two years before I came along, I thought that he was way out of the picture by this point. Once Maya devoted herself to me, I expected complete transparency from her. What I saw in those few seconds was totally inappropriate to me and I had to make a swift decision about what to do once Maya returned from the bathroom.

There are two types of people in the world when it comes to an unexpected situation like this. The first type would carefully place their partner's phone back where it was picked up and pretend that they didn't see anything. Maybe the topic will be sensitively brought up for a discussion later in the future, or never brought up at all because of the fear of what it may cost. The second type would stand their ground, hold on to that phone, and display it for their partner to see as soon as they return. I chose to go with the latter and I confronted Maya right then and there.

No matter how hard I tried, it simply wasn't in my nature to beat around the bush and act as if this was alright in any way. Of course, an argument ensued that was much louder and belligerent than the one in the coffee shop right now.

Maya stormed out of my place in tears, and I was left alone to ponder about what could happen from here on out. I should've ended our relationship that very night, but a piece of me somehow convinced myself to stay, fight, and hold on to what we had. In some weird way, I didn't want to abandon Maya like how other people had always abandoned me so easily. I didn't want this one moment to ruin what we'd built up over the past few months with love and support.

We make millions of decisions throughout our life and a handful of those drastically change our path. It's always been much easier for humans to fight with one other instead of being able to forgive. I wanted to change that, so I stuck by Maya's side and we made it up to each other in weeks that followed. I knew it was wrong of me to go through her personal property like I did, and it was even worse for her to go behind my back to message her ex-boyfriend. However, we gradually rebuilt our mutual respect and gained level ground again, agreeing to leave the past behind us.

Either I was the biggest fool in the universe or there was a sliver of hope for rekindling our initial spark and repairing our relationship.

"You're the paranoid one in this relationship and always have been," Maya says, as my focus is diverted back to the coffee shop dispute. "You've always had trust issues and they keep coming in between us. I honestly can't do this anymore."

"I have those issues because of YOU! And you're not doing anything to help. You're making me sound like the bad guy when it's you who's being the manipulative one. The things that you said and did made me feel like you wanted go back to him," Past Danny says. "You should've stopped your little interactions with him, but you didn't!"

I remember that our dented love story continued for months after the text message incident and things were looking relatively good again. I thought that Maya was special because of the way she made me laugh and enjoy life. She was there for me when I needed someone to talk to and I was open with her. While we naturally still bickered here and there, it wasn't anything as serious as the night with the text messages.

With that said, my mind had the seeds of doubt sowed into it and I couldn't dig them out. I was inherently stuck in the middle of my conflicting thoughts with an angel on one shoulder and a devil on the other. Despite my internal contradictions, I continued to hope for the best and I did whatever I could to maintain a healthy relationship. I've always believed that true love isn't measured by the amount of good times you enjoy in each other's presence, but more so by the amount of bad times you effectively overcome together. Being able to stick with each other throughout the lowest of lows like a devoted team is the utmost quality a couple can strive for.

As time went on, I left most of my skepticism behind me and I tried showing more appreciation for what I had. I ended up saving enough money for an engagement ring to make us truly official and begin the next chapter of our lives together.

Looking back at it now, it was a rather hasty decision on my part. It was as if I was trying to fix all my deeply rooted problems while simultaneously fast-tracking my way to the happiness that I thought I deserved. The truth is that happiness is something that can't be chased. Instead, it's earned as a by-product from what you're doing and how you're living. I should've allowed my notion of happiness to arrive on its own instead of quickly betting all my hopes for it on an engagement ring and getting married.

"It wasn't any of your business to begin with because I told you it didn't mean anything. But you kept prying anyway and look at us now," Maya says to Past Danny in the coffee shop.

"None of my business? What my fiancé does is none of my business? What world are you living in?" Past Danny asks.

"Whoever I text, follow on social media, or see in person shouldn't even matter to you. You literally have me all to yourself and you're still so doubtful," Maya says.

"It's because you give me all the reasons to be. When have you ever seen me being as secretive as you? At least I tell you where I'm going or where I'm at as a bare minimum," Past Danny says.

The heated exchange continues and I'm feeling the same range of emotions that Past Danny is currently feeling. Equal parts of anger mixed in with sadness is a concoction that doesn't feel pleasant at all.

I'm watching my former relationship crumble before me and there's nothing I can possibly do or say that'll save it. The very foundation of this relationship has eroded and it's not so easily replaceable.

My eyes roll over to the wooden table in the centre of Past Danny and Maya. They become fixed on the engagement ring sitting right in the middle of it. Something so small, a few millimetres in diameter, contains so much meaning and significance. It represents many aspects of a relationship, but most of all it represents trust. However, correlating trust with a physical ring is much different than acquiring trust in the first place and maintaining it.

When I placed that ring on Maya's finger by the shore during a picturesque sunset overlooking Lake Ontario, I thought that it was our defining moment and nothing else would come in our way. I had known her for over a year at that point, which I thought was enough time to get to know someone inside out. I didn't have the patience to wait a few more years and pop the question when I would be well into my thirties. Instead of focusing on my present, I kept thinking about my future and how I would be a better dad than mine ever was.

As the old children's story goes, *slow and steady wins the race.* That's something I should've followed a bit more closely.

"Whatever you're accusing me of now is an all-time low for you. I told you I went to go see a friend and for some reason, you don't believe me. I'm done trying to convince you and I'm done with you. Take your ring and tell your parents that I'm not interested anymore. I don't care what they say about me, there's no saving us!" Maya says in a loud tone.

"I wouldn't have accused you of anything if you were just honest with me from the start!" Past Danny replies in an even louder tone. "You've been nothing but a liar!"

Emotions are erupting like lava from an unstable volcano. The other people sitting in the coffee shop are now glancing over at this table every few seconds to see what's going on.

I remember a few weeks after we got engaged, I was casually scrolling through my social media followers to get a rough idea of who we could invite to our wedding. After making my list, I then proceeded to go through Maya's followers as well. As I scrolled down, whatever remaining confidence I had in our relationship was ruined.

One of Maya's followers appeared to be the exact same person who she was texting all those months ago when I caught her red-handed. I knew for a fact that she wasn't following her ex-boyfriend on social media back then so out of further suspicion, I clicked on his profile. I confirmed that it was the same individual named Zaire.

My blood began to boil as my heart sank to its bottom. Why would Maya casually follow him and allow him to follow her back? I was never really against the idea that lovers could remain friends after they've split. However, that theory was officially thrown out the window once I found those initial text messages and from what I stumbled across once more. There had to have been something going on between them that I didn't know about.

I was distraught but I attempted a quieter strategy this time around. I didn't confront Maya right away like last time but instead, I opted to show some patience and gather more evidence.

A few days passed and I received a text message from Maya. She told me that she couldn't come over to my place on our scheduled Friday evening because she had made another plan to hang out at a friend's house instead. She usually wasn't one to cancel plans between us, so I thought this was an odd change out of the blue. I said it was alright for her to go and I told her to enjoy her night.

In my anxious state of mind, I knew that this was an opportunity to confirm my suspicions. I proceeded to search online for a private investigator to help me uncover the truth about all these doubts torturing my conscience. I didn't know anyone who had ever done this before and I thought it only happened in movies. Yet here I was, forcing myself to do the one thing that I thought I'd never have to do: spy on my fiancé.

I found a private investigator for a reasonable price, and I instructed him to tail Maya once she had left her house on that Friday evening. The investigator's name was Frank, a middle-aged man who used to be a police officer and had extensive experience from doing this type of work before. He reassured me that this was nothing to be embarrassed about and that I'd be surprised at how many people hired private investigators nowadays to settle their worries about their partners.

Frank told me to relax while he got the job done and kept saying that I was in great hands. He was a confident guy and to be honest, I trusted him more than I did Maya on that night. Professional camera in hand, Frank left to go to work on my behalf and I threw on a movie to watch. As I sat on the couch by myself, my thoughts were transfixed on Maya and I hoped that my worst fears wouldn't come to pass. I eventually went to sleep thinking about how tomorrow would either make or break my relationship.

The next morning, Frank rang my doorbell and I invited him inside. He sat on the couch while I made two cups of coffee.

Once the formality and small talk was over, it was time for me to know what happened.

"Well Danny, I don't know how to say this to you... She didn't end up going to any friend's place last night."

I'll never forget my heart shattering into a million pieces when I heard Frank say that. All my haunting suspicions had been confirmed by a third party with solid proof.

Frank placed all the photographs he took from the previous night on the table in front of me. They displayed the entire chain of events from beginning to end. With each photo that I viewed, I wanted to throw up. They showed everything from Maya leaving her house, getting in her car, driving to a restaurant by the lake, eating dinner and having drinks on the patio with Zaire, getting back in her car, following him into his house, and then finally leaving two hours later.

I felt damaged beyond repair, like a car that had been instantly totaled from a head-on collision. I tried to hold back my tears as best as I could, but I felt utterly humiliated and betrayed. A few tears slipped past my eyelids and Frank noticed. He placed his hand on my shoulder and told me that everything would be alright, as well as how great of a guy I was. His final words to me before he left my home were similar to something Peri would've said.

"Life always finds a way to work things out. There's someone else out there for you who'll cross your path one day."

Why was it that whenever I found some temporary happiness, an eternity of disappointment and distress followed right after? The universe was perpetually challenging me and pushing me beyond my limits instead of letting me live a life in peace.

After Frank left, I texted Maya and told her that I knew she didn't go to her "friend's" place last night. She was oblivious to my words at first, and she kept up her innocent act to make me look like a fool. We argued over text messages for a while before I told her to meet me at the local coffee shop, where I would spill everything and put an end to this nightmare. Texting paragraphs doesn't always convey the most accurate of feelings, so I wanted to do it face-to-face and be somewhat civil for a final farewell. The result of that decision and expectation is what's playing out in front of me now.

"This is the last time I'm saying this. I went to visit a friend from college. She was dealing with family drama and needed someone to talk to. I'll give you her phone number so you can ask her yourself. If you still don't believe me, then whatever. That's on you," Maya says like a true devil in disguise. She's beautiful on the outside but rotten to her core on the inside.

Past Danny smirks and then sighs. I feel the same suffering he's enduring as he tries his absolute best to keep his composure. He stares at Maya as if she'll voice some sort of last-minute atonement for her actions.

All the inappropriate text messages, the unnecessary social media follow, and the blatant lying to sneak off behind my back. Technically, Maya had already gotten three strikes and she was out. Yet in this very moment, I *still* gave her a subtle fourth and final chance to prove her worth to me.

A few seconds passed and as I expected, Maya didn't budge and her face didn't show a shred of remorse. With that signal, Past Danny takes out the photos taken by Frank from his coat pocket and places them on the table next to the engagement ring.

I didn't want to attain some sense of revenge or pleasure from doing this, but I knew it had to be done otherwise I could never forgive myself.

"What's this?" Maya asks, finally showing some vulnerability and nervousness in her tone. The phrase, *like a deer caught in the headlights*, couldn't have been more applicable.

Maya only views three photos before realizing there's no chance of defending herself, so she goes on the offensive instead.

"Are you serious right now? How could you do this? You have no right… YOU'RE A CRAZY PSYCHO!" Maya shouts in his face while pointing her finger at him.

"And you're a filthy cheater," Past Danny replies. "Enjoy the rest of your life."

I watch Maya explode up from her seat and the table violently shakes, almost flipping over. She looks right at Past Danny with tears in her eyes.

I didn't expect any apology from Maya because I knew she was angrier at the fact that she got caught instead of being angry at herself.

Maya proves my point when she viciously slaps Past Danny on his left cheek with so much force that it leaves a clear red imprint. She then storms out of the coffee shop and slams the door behind her.

Everyone in the establishment is aware of what took place. A barista walks over to Past Danny and asks him if he's alright. My past self replies by nodding. At the same time, Peri walks over in a similar fashion and sits in an empty chair beside me.

"I'm sorry about this Danny," Peri says.

I observe everyone around us in the coffee shop and they're all staring at my past self. They've most likely created their own judgements and theories about what happened. They can try to interpret what they witnessed all they want but they'll never understand the underlying issues unless they experience it for themselves.

I wish I could take the time to explain to everyone here that I gave that relationship my all, but it was of no effect. Better yet, I wish I could tell them the truth that I bet everything on this one relationship to relieve my inherent depression, even though I always had a gut feeling that it was doomed from the start.

Would I have still asked Maya to marry me if I wasn't suffering from depression? I highly doubt it. I got so caught up in trying to chase happiness that that I ended up receiving nothing but sorrow. I knew that I deserved someone so much better than Maya but because of my irrational choices, this traumatizing event only made my internal conflict worse.

I stare at my past self while he blankly stares at the door of the entrance. It's like he's daydreaming about what could've happened if his fiancé had simply been faithful to him. Instead, I feel his deep embarrassment, frustration, regret, anger, and sadness.

"You must think I have the worst life possible by now," I say to Peri.

"That's not true Danny," Peri replies. "Everyone's life is different with its own challenges."

"It seems like I always ended up getting the short end of the stick," I say.

"These experiences are a part of life, whether you want to encounter them or not," Peri says. "Of course, there's many people out there who are lucky enough to avoid any tragedy or loss… Like people who find love at first sight and live happily ever after. On the other hand, I've seen people suffer unbearable pain… Like when more than one partner cheats on them."

The heartbreak of one partner doing this to me is enough to crumble my spirit. I could never imagine this happening to me multiple times. If that was the case, I would permanently lose all my hope and give up trying to find a companion for the rest of my life.

"How could Maya have the audacity to do that to me? I didn't do or say anything wrong to her ever since I knew her," I say. "I was always open with everything and I wanted the best for us. What did I do to deserve that?"

"Think of it this way…" Peri starts. "It's better that you found out about Maya's intentions sooner rather than later. Imagine if she continued to be disloyal and dishonest for months, even *years*, without you knowing. How devastating that would've been."

Peri does have a point. You either rip the bandage off your wound right away or you can peel it back slowly and prolong the inevitable. This entire situation is difficult to comprehend because I never expected it to happen to me of all people.

I thought that I had been through enough suffering in my life and that I paid my dues. I thought it was finally time to relax and enjoy my life with someone else, as if a long-term relationship would be a vacation from reality. It turned out to be nothing more than another dark chapter within the depressing saga of my life.

The greatest setback is when you realize all the time and effort you poured into a relationship without receiving anything back. You invest all your hopes and dreams into this significant other like an appreciating stock but all you end up with is a negative return. You can keep waiting to see if it'll ever bounce back to its previous highs or you can take the loss and try to move on with your life. Accepting that loss may be feasible but coping with that loss afterward is another hurdle altogether.

"Can we move on? I really don't want to be here anymore," I say to Peri. I want to get out of this memory sequence more than anything now.

I can't help but think about the hopelessness that filled me after this undesirable episode in the coffee shop. Even though I was lied to and betrayed by my fiancé, I still told Maya to enjoy the rest of her life when I spoke my final words to her. I always wished positivity for others while I continued to be demoralized with each life event that passed me by. It was a trait within me that I profoundly resented.

Once Maya slapped me and walked out that door, I felt like my trust in humanity left with her. The trust that I had in my dad, in my teachers, in my friends, and in my fiancé withered away over time and it didn't get me anywhere. From here on out, my goal was to solely focus on myself first and eliminate my inner desire to depend on other people for anything again. The only person I could trust now was myself and myself alone.

"Remember Danny, try to control your emotions even if it seems impossible. Good times will always follow the bad times in your life. You've seen that with your own eyes, and you've made it this far," Peri says.

"To tell you the truth right now, there's a huge part of me that doesn't want to move on. If this is what my life was really like before I ended up in the forest, is it even worth going back to?" I ask.

"That's a question that I can't answer for you. My task is to guide you and give you the tools to help you make that decision for yourself. You have to determine what's best for you in the end," Peri says.

I look at Past Danny moving his chair backward from the table beside us. He gets up, collects the engagement ring and photos sitting on top of the table, and proceeds to walk to the entrance of the coffee shop. Before Past Danny exits, he dumps all the evidence of Maya's night out into the garbage bin beside the door. He then walks out into the pouring rain with his umbrella and becomes one with the herd of pedestrians.

I can't remember anything beyond a few weeks past this memory, but I'm sure that I became an embittered man for a long time. I feel nothing but the heaviest of agony within my mind. It would take an absolute miracle for me to be able to trust anyone else again. Here's to hoping that whatever memory Peri shows me next will somehow change my cynical mentality.

"Let's finish this door then. I need to know what happened after this," I say as I get up from my chair.

Peri nods his head, stands up, and holds out his hand in front of him. He snaps his fingers, and the coffee shop disintegrates before us. The floor, aroma, antique clock on the wall, chairs, and tables all dissipates into nothingness.

I'm standing back in the lifeless void from where I started this door and I close my eyes. I feel the glimmer working away and creating a new environment around me. My thoughts are entirely consumed with Maya and her boldness to go so far behind my back. I try to think about something else to distract my mind but no luck. A partner's betrayal can make even the toughest of people fall by decimating them from the inside out.

As I open my eyes, the new environment has almost taken shape and is much more expansive than the coffee shop. There's something vastly different happening this time around, unlike any one of the previous memories. This environment around me and Peri isn't static but instead, it's in constant motion.

"You may want to stand next to me for this one," Peri says.

I do as Peri instructs and walk over to him to stand by his side. Suddenly, the remaining glimmer that's hovering nearby begins to encircle us extra closely. It creates a mold directly beneath us, above us, and around us. It's not long before I realize that we're being forced into a sitting position as the glimmer presses us into the backseat of a moving car. The glimmer then stops moving and it fills up with vivid colours, which is the signal that this new environment has been officially completed.

I first notice all the green grass and scattered white lines on the road whipping past us as I stare outside of this car window to my left.

"Well, this is new," I say to Peri, who's sitting on my right.

"Strap on your seatbelt," Peri teases.

I continue to stare out of the window of this moving car. There's a magnificent display of nature with tall trees gently moving with the wind, the sun shining overhead, a bright blue sky, and squirrels bouncing around going about their day. After the gloomy weather outside of the coffee shop, as well as the gloomier atmosphere that was experienced within it, this is a sight for sore eyes. I redirect my attention to two people who are sitting in the front seats, an arm's length away.

The seat on the right, in front of Peri, has a woman sitting in it who I can't recognize. If this happens to be Maya again, I may as well jump out of the moving car right now. Next to her in the driver's seat has to be my past self. I glance into the rear-view mirror to get a better look at his eyes, hoping for a dead giveaway again. He's wearing a pair of sunglasses with golden frames so that strategy doesn't work this time. As I'm about to learn forward out of my seat to investigate his face, I fall back when he begins to speak out loud.

The tone of your voice never seems to be the way you envision it in your head. It's weird to hear yourself speak from a recorded video, but it's even more bizarre when you're hearing yourself speak right in front of you.

"There's a nice spot coming up where we can stop and take a break," Past Danny says with his stylish sunglasses on.

"Sounds good, let's do it!" the lady replies.

I know her voice from somewhere, but I can't put a name to it. I'll find out soon enough when this memory pours back into my mind.

"I haven't been here in a long time," Past Danny continues.

"I've never been here at all! The views are wonderful so far," the lady says.

"I'm glad you're having fun and enjoying it," Past Danny says.

I stare out of the window again to admire the gorgeous sight. I catch sporadic glimpses of Lake Ontario through the thick trees. There's something about that lake that always holds my attention, no matter which angle I look at it from and no matter how old

I get. The natural, quiet, and serene beauty of it is unsurpassed, even despite my pathetic memory of proposing to Maya right next to it.

I've always felt more comfortable within nature than I ever did within a big city. Large concrete structures built by people are impressive, but they can't compare to the marvelous creations of Mother Earth. I recall the trip with Sylvia and James to New York City all those years ago. While it was fun to visit for a few days, I couldn't picture myself living there for good. The immense crowds of people, nonstop traffic, and the constant hustle and bustle lifestyle simply wasn't for me. I believe that there's just as much beauty within simplicity. There's a unique story to be told with each blade of grass, each trunk of a tree, and each ripple of water.

"I've seen many places, all with their own sights, sounds, and wonders. But yours is special in its own way," Peri says. "You're lucky to live in a place where no matter which direction you wander off, you're bound to discover something new."

"It's usually taken for granted. Most people here don't step outside their comfort zone to experience a bit of nature," I say.

The car is now travelling up a steep hill and with each second it climbs, it's as if we're leaving earth to go to space. The car pushes forward for a few more minutes before the road finally flattens out and the car becomes level again. We're surrounded by dense trees on both sides of us and I can't see anything past them. They're eerily similar to the trees in the forest that I'm trying to escape.

This can't be the same place, can it? Even if it is, it wouldn't make a difference. All of this is an illusion and strictly a means to an end.

Past Danny slows the car down and takes a left turn on a barely visible dirt road. Up ahead on this shabby road, there's an area that resembles a small, worn-out parking lot on top of a dirt patch. There are no other cars occupying any of the minimal spaces, so this must be some secluded area. Past Danny stops and parks the car in one of the empty spots. The trees virtually surround us from every direction here, except for a tiny opening near us that you could walk through.

"Hey, let me check if this is the same spot," Past Danny says to the lady.

"Don't worry, I'm not going anywhere," she replies with a smile.

Past Danny opens his door and gets out of the car. I do the same, almost as if I'm imitating him. He's wearing blue jeans with a red polo shirt. Past Danny strides past the car and the dirt parking lot. He then enters the tiny opening, which contains a very narrow dirt path, and begins to walk past the obstruction of trees. I follow right behind him, and we continue onward for a few more seconds.

Past Danny exits out of this natural corridor, takes a few more steps forward, and finally stops walking. As I make it out of the same opening, there's an entire vista unfolding in front of my eyes. The scenery keeps expanding and getting better with each step that I take. I arrive beside Past Danny and words can't express how remarkable this new view is.

If picture perfect was a place, this would be it. We're standing atop a high peak that must be hundreds of metres above the ground from where we came. I walk close to the edge to look down below and there are thousands of trees covering the landscape. On my left, I can see the road that we were just travelling on. It stretches as far back into the sloped distance as I can see, all the way to the Skyway Bridge.

I squint my eyes to get a better look at what's in front of me. I can see the outline of Toronto's downtown core, right on the other side of Lake Ontario. The city is far off in the distance but the CN Tower is easily distinguishable, standing tall and proud within it. No matter where I am, that tower will always act as a beacon for my home here in Canada. On my right, the rest of Lake Ontario stretches far off into the horizon, as if it's an endless oasis of water with the sunlight shining down on it. There's also a small picnic table on this peak, which isn't exactly safe being this close to the edge but it's worth it for the view. Someone must've brought it over once before and left it here for others to enjoy.

Past Danny walks over to this picnic table, taps it twice, smiles, and begins to jog back through the opening in the trees. I stay where I am, and I can hear my past self shouting from the dirt path.

"Jessica! Over here! This is the spot. You can come on out now!" Past Danny yells out loud.

As soon as Past Danny says her name, I feel the swarm of memories rushing back into my mind. All my memories since the coffee shop, especially the good ones, hit my system like a vaccine intended for an incurable disease. I take a seat at the picnic table in complete bliss, as the plaguing memory of Maya shrivels far away into the back of my mind and no longer concerns me.

At the forefront of my mind is the irresistible excitement, happiness, and satisfaction that Past Danny is feeling in this very moment. I remember that this was one of the best experiences I ever had in my life. Fantastic views, perfect weather, peace, quiet, and an entire day spent with Jessica, the former receptionist from the children's hospital. This is one of those times that helped propel me back to my normal self, or at least closer to it.

"This is amazing Danny!" Jessica says as she walks out of the opening behind Past Danny. She's wearing a floral dress and has a huge grin on her face with a picnic basket in her hand.

Peri also follows through, and he observes this view for himself before approaching me.

"This is a sight to behold, no doubt about it. Which city are we close to?" Peri asks.

"I'm not entirely sure. From what I remember, we're not too far away from a town called Grimsby," I say.

"That name sounds different, I like it. *Grimsby*," Peri repeats with a smile.

Jessica sets the picnic basket on top of the table and proceeds to open it up. She unloads some sandwiches, strawberries, blueberries, grapes, salads, cold cuts, crackers, and cheese.

"Ah, that reminds me. Hold on a minute, I'll be back!" Past Danny tells Jessica as she's laying the food out.

"Stop running away from me!" she jokes.

Past Danny jogs back to the car to retrieve something he forgot while Peri and I continue to admire the beauty around us. A few moments later, Past Danny returns with some items strategically held up behind his back.

I remember exactly what they are.

He slowly walks over to the picnic table before unveiling his surprise.

"What's this Danny? You didn't have to!" Jessica says.

"I remembered you mentioning that it was your birthday last week, but you were busy working and didn't get to do anything," Past Danny says. He's holding out a bottle of red wine, two delicate-looking wine glasses, and a little chocolate birthday cake. "I thought we'd celebrate it now," Past Danny says with a smile.

"Aw, you're so sweet Danny. Thank you! This means so much to me," Jessica says.

Peri looks at me with a smirk on his face.

"I guess you finally improved your flirting skills," Peri says.

"Alright, alright, relax… I was just being nice," I reply unconvincingly.

Past Danny opens the bottle of wine while standing, and he pours an even amount of the red liquid in both wine glasses. He holds his glass up before saying happy birthday to Jessica. She clinks her wine glass with his and they both take a sip.

"Let's get started then," Past Danny says as he takes a seat.

I get up from the picnic table and take a few steps away from Past Danny and Jessica. They're both sitting across from each other and begin digging into their food.

"So…" Jessica says after eating a few bites. "What took you so long to ask me to hang out? I swear you've been in and out of the hospital for years."

"I don't know, I'm sorry. So much has happened since we first met. From being busy with school to trying to find work, moving out, dealing with life…" Past Danny continues.

I made everything seem so insignificant and small, thinking that it was better to tell her less instead of more. I couldn't spill my guts and tell her that my spirit was crumbling in the years following our college days.

"We should've hung out a long time ago so that's on me. I'll take the blame. But here we are now!" Past Danny says as he slightly raises his arms. "Anyway, I see that you didn't have to move very far for your new job."

"To be honest, I still can't believe it. Going from a front desk receptionist to a nurse within the same hospital. I never thought I'd end up getting placed there. It's become a second home to me now," Jessica says.

"That's awesome, I'm really proud of you," Past Danny says as he eats a strawberry.

It's nice to see that I eventually overcame my setback with Maya and moved on with my life, even if this was only a small trip with Jessica as friends. Following the disaster in the coffee shop, I once again isolated myself from everyone and was pretty much a wreck for a year afterward. I felt like I couldn't trust anyone anymore, so my social life became nonexistent. Despite my depressing thoughts, there was still a piece of me deep inside that knew I needed to get out and explore the world again, but I had no idea where to start.

There came a day, shortly after I had turned 30, when I decided to stop by the children's hospital after an extremely long hiatus. Like the old days, I felt like visiting some kids who may not have gotten any visitors in a while and provide them company. The hospital had previously gotten me out of my slump after the incident with Bella, so I thought it would somehow do it again after what happened with Maya.

The children's hospital did end up helping me, but not in the way that I was expecting. When I walked into the hospital that day and I didn't see Jessica at the front desk, I thought that she'd finally flown from this nest and found work somewhere else. Part of me was sad because I had gotten so used to seeing her greet me with kindness, while the other part of me was happy for her and I hoped that she found her dream job. I greeted the new receptionist, signed the visitor log, and waited in front of the elevator doors to go up like I always did. As both the doors slid open to their opposing ends, there stood Jessica right in front of me wearing a nurse's uniform.

The excitement instantly lit our faces up and we agreed to meet after her shift was done, where we then struck up a lengthy conversation and caught up like old friends. That was also my perfect chance to ask her to go out for a friendly outing on her day off, which I desperately needed more than ever.

She happily agreed and now here we are days later, enjoying each other's company as if two long lost friends have been reunited. It's an unexpected but pleasant surprise when a person who's always been in the background of your life suddenly moves to the foreground. Someone who should've had more of your attention from the beginning but didn't receive it until months, or in this case, years later. Life always seems to work in mysterious ways like that, for better or for worse. In this specific moment, it was most definitely the former. I was in complete ecstasy from finding someone to socialize with again and that too, Jessica of all people.

Jessica pulls out her phone and starts to show Past Danny pictures from the children's hospital, which brings a huge smile to their faces. She's always been a beautiful person inside out, with a smile that makes my heart throb.

I walk over to Peri, who's standing at the edge of the peak and enjoying the sights from this height. I join him and we both observe nature's beauty together.

"This was much needed… Thank you for allowing me to relive this moment," I say.

"As I said earlier Danny, a good memory will always follow a bad one, no matter how horrible you think it is," Peri replies.

"One of my problems has always been that these *good* memories aren't as frequent as I'd like them to be. They're too far apart from one another. They can take weeks, months, or even years to appear. It's like I have to chase after the good times while the bad times are relentlessly chasing after me," I say.

"Not everything can be handed to us on a platter," Peri says. "There are times when we can get lucky, but most times we have to work for what we want and that can take longer than usual. Take this memory for instance. If you hadn't left your isolation and asked Jessica to hang out with you, this memory wouldn't even exist. It was a simple question but because of it, you experienced an incredible view with an incredible person that you'll never forget. All it took was a little bit of courage."

I start thinking about all the times I purposely stayed locked away from everyone else, like I checked myself into solitary confinement. How many more positive memories did I miss out on because of my decision to stay isolated whenever I got hurt? Most likely too many to count.

"I want you to make me a promise Danny," Peri says.

I turn toward him as he's staring at the majestic lake in the distance. I'm curious about what he's about to request from me.

"What is it?" I ask.

"Promise me that no matter what else happens throughout your life, you'll always try to keep your head up. That no matter how down and out you may feel, you'll always pick yourself back up and push forward," Peri says. He extends his hand out with the intention to shake mine, just like he did at the shore when we first met each other.

If there's anything I've learned throughout this journey with Peri, it's that there'll always be positivity somewhere in the world to counteract all the negativity. Optimism can prevail over pessimism if you allow it to. The good times in life may take a while to arrive after the difficult times, but they'll eventually be there for you to experience. All it takes is a little bit of patience and hope.

I confidently extend my hand out to Peri and we shake on it.

"I promise I'll always try my best and not give up, no matter what life hurls at me," I say.

"Good man," Peri says to me like a proud parent. "So anyway, whatever happened with Jessica after this little date?"

I take a few seconds to think about what followed this excursion. I can only remember everything up until about a month later, and it's not the result I was expecting.

"This wasn't exactly a date… We were just hanging out as friends. I don't think we went out again after this," I admit.

"Well, why not?" Peri asks.

"Looking back at it now, I'm not sure. I guess I didn't want to take another chance and risk opening myself up to another girl again. It's not that I didn't like Jessica, because I really admired her. It's that I forgot how to trust others as much as I used to," I say.

"Do yourself a favour and reach out to her again once you're out of this place," Peri says. "It's impossible to predict who's worthy of our trust until we actually decide to trust them."

Peri looks back at Jessica and Past Danny laughing together while drinking their wine. They're still viewing old photos on her phone and it's overloading them with joy.

"Also, at least this one isn't afraid to show you her phone," Peri teases with a smirk.

"Okay Mr. Matchmaker, I'll think about it," I say.

My mind keeps telling me I should've seen Jessica again soon after this day. At that time, I became too caught up with bigger ideas related to long-term commitment and marriage that I didn't stop to realize that those aren't the only things that matter when you're seeing someone. I could've at least kept in touch as a close friend as I rebuilt my inner strength from the ground up. Instead, I treated it like a one-and-done situation where this single interaction was enough for me.

"I should've told her how I felt. I really needed a friend, but I didn't want to show it," I say.

"We can't all be as carefree as these birds flying around in the sky. I know you have what it takes to become the best version of you," Peri says. "Don't be afraid to open up to others. There's still a lot of good people in this world."

As Past Danny and Jessica are enjoying every second of their time together, I'm feeling the same sense of comfort, warmth, and enjoyment in that very moment. It's the opposite of the tense, cold, bitter, and gloomy feeling I had from the last memory in the coffee shop. If only this moment atop this peak could last forever. Why do all good things eventually come to an end?

I prevent myself from wandering any further with that thought. I have to train myself to avoid that question altogether and learn to find solace within these particular moments instead. Good times are not beautiful because they last, they're beautiful because they happened.

"I'll find her when I get back," I say.

"Glad to hear it," Peri replies, as we continue to gaze at the horizon of this breathtaking landscape.

All of a sudden, a flashing sound rings in our ears from somewhere behind us. I quickly turn around to check where it came from.

Nothing directly around us, and nothing from the table where Past Danny and Jessica are sitting. Out of curiosity, I walk over to the opening in the trees and take a few steps in to look at the car. There's the culprit. The interior of the car is completely glowing from a bright white light to the point where the seats aren't visible. This is the strangest portal yet, but it makes sense considering there's no door to be found here and exit from. I walk back to Peri to notify him.

"The car is all lit up from the inside," I say.

"That's our cue, we should get going. Time is ticking away," Peri says.

"What can I expect from the final door?" I ask before we make a move.

"If I told you now, it would defeat the purpose," Peri replies.

"Could you at least give me a hint? What if I can't handle it?" I ask.

"I'm sorry Danny, I can't do that. But I know you'll be okay from what I've seen so far. I have faith in you," Peri says.

I feel slightly reassured, and I try not to think too much about what awaits me. I have to ride this journey out until the very end and whatever happens, happens.

"Let's go then," I say.

We walk by my past self and Jessica, who are revelling in their spirited conversation in the most serene of places. I feel happy that I was able to give myself a break and go out on an adventure like this, especially with someone as lovely as Jessica. I hope I'm able to survive this ordeal and see her again one day. If I do, I'll bring her back here and ask her to be my girlfriend.

Peri and I walk through the opening in the trees and use the dirt path to reach the parking lot. We then walk toward the car, which is now our portal to get back to the forest.

"After you," Peri says.

I swing one of the doors open as Past Danny left the car unlocked when he came to collect the wine and birthday cake. The light shines out of the car as bright as the sun, which is how it always appears when we leave through a door. I proceed to sit inside the backseat of the car and shuffle over as Peri follows me in and the light surrounds me.

Once I'm fully adjusted and Peri closes the door behind him, the white light fills in all the spaces around us until I can no longer make out a single detail inside or outside of the car. The light engulfs me with its brightness and warm sensation as I close my eyes. There's one more door left and it's time to find out what's behind it.

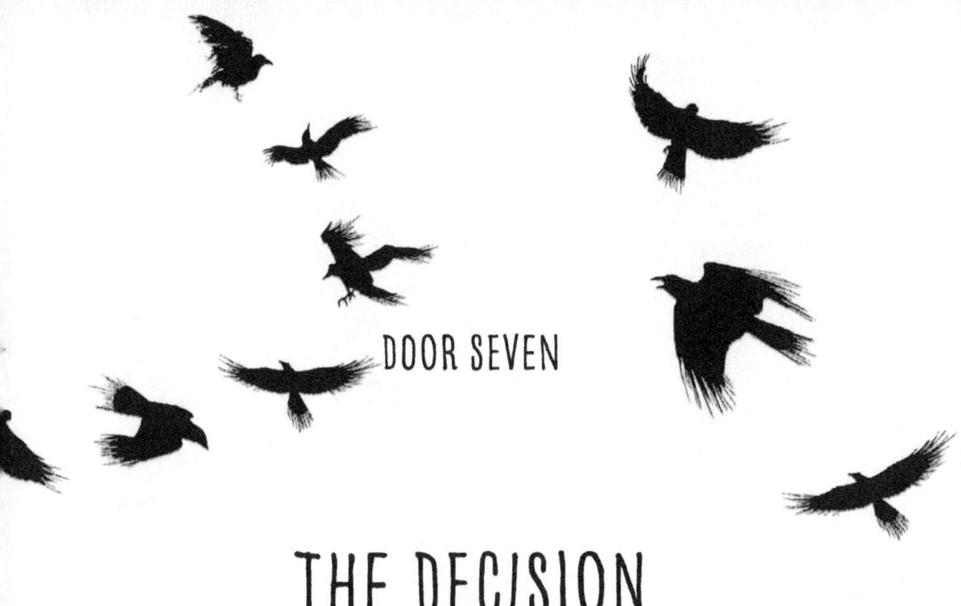

THE DECISION

Peri vigorously shakes my body on the ground as I awaken and regain my senses.

"Get up Danny, there's not a lot of time left," Peri says.

Once I realize we're back in the forest, I quickly get up and compose myself. The fog has approached far enough to pose a real danger from every direction. This clearing that was once large has now shrunk to the size of a garden and it continues to diminish in size with each passing second.

"Is there any way to get rid of it?" I ask. I walk over to the edge of the remaining ground and raise my arm toward the fog.

"Get away from it! Don't let it touch you! Enter the last door *now* and once you've seen what you need to see, your trial will be complete. You'll be safe and free to go back to where you came from," Peri says.

I retreat to a safe distance and then look up at the night sky. The crows are croaking loudly, like they're ready to rip my soul away and feast on it. As heavy as my body feels and as much as I want to sit down to take a break from everything, I know that I have to make one final push.

"I'm ready to go," I say.

"No matter what you encounter in this door, remember how far you've come in your life," Peri says. "All the bad times you've been through, all the people who've hurt you, all the self-imposed guilt… There's always something better waiting for you on the other side."

Peri's words instill a sense of confidence within me but at the same time, make me worried. If this door has saved my worst memory for last, I'm not sure I'll make it out of here alive. I hope for the best possible outcome and commit to finishing the task.

"Thank you for helping me get this far," I say. "I won't forget it."

Peri nods his head, and we walk toward the seventh and final door of this grueling quest that's almost at its end. The fog steadily approaches with each second that I waste. I place my right hand on the doorknob and swing the glowing door open. I step into the dark void with Peri behind me. He closes the door with the fog and crows disappearing out of my view and out of my mind, at least for now.

Is this truly the last time I'll have to endure any mental anguish? When this is all over, will I feel like I've attained salvation or will it have been for nothing? All I can do now is wait to uncover my fate.

The glimmer shapes the new environment around me and Peri. I've often forgotten that this entire space is only a simulation because of how real everything appears to be. It's near identical to real life, so my urge to escape this false labyrinth is at the forefront of my thoughts.

The glimmer begins to slow down and fill in the final spots of the scene, before finishing it off by injecting colour into it. This environment seems to be a small park within a city, during the evening as the sun is setting. The sky is a unique blend of yellow, orange, red, and purple. I can see some buildings far off in the distance, along with two roads that meet each other to create a small intersection.

We're standing on a concrete walkway that encircles the entire park, which contains a white-coloured gazebo in the middle of it. There are trees spread around us with bright green leaves on their tall branches and plentiful flowers by the bottom of their trunks to compliment them. This seems to be some time in the summer. There's also a small playground outside of the walkway, where kids are energetically running around and playing with each other. Peri and I begin to walk around to get a bearing of our surroundings. There's a brown metallic sign close to us that has some words written on it. *Gage Park. Open Since 1903.*

"I know where we are," I say to Peri. "This is downtown Brampton. When I moved out of my parents' house, I often came back to visit this park. I would sit on one of the benches and reminisce about growing up in this city."

"Lovely place Danny. Your past self must be around here somewhere then. Don't forget, we're on the clock," Peri says.

I begin striding faster toward the area that I used to sit in when my mom would bring me here as a young boy. There's a man sitting on a bench beside the walkway in that same area. He's facing inward to the gazebo and the trees around it. He seems to be working on something with a pencil and a notebook in his hand. That has to be me sitting there.

The man is wearing blue jeans with a black shirt and dark green jacket over top of it. I approach the figure's front side to view his face and my theory is confirmed.

There's something unusual that makes me step back for a moment. I pull out my phone from my pocket and stare at the glass screen to view my reflection within it. Throughout all the previous memories, I felt like I was looking at a former shadow of myself. I'd gotten used to seeing my past self as a child, a teenager, and a young adult. However, the person sitting in front of me shows absolutely no distinction in age. The resemblance has caught up to the point where my past self is indistinguishable from my current appearance.

"I don't understand… That's exactly how I look right now. How long ago was this?" I ask Peri.

"Not too long ago," Peri says.

I'm trying my hardest to remember what happened on this evening and for the life of me, I don't have the faintest idea. I feel like I'm missing the final one percent of my memory before I'm finally caught up to where I am now.

I stare at Past Danny as if I'm looking right into a mirror. He continues to write in his little notebook with his pencil. Peri and I remain by his side as he sits alone in this park.

Past Danny's phone suddenly alerts him of an incoming text message with a small beeping tone. He's using the exact same phone that I pulled out of my pocket. Everything else from his hair to his stubble beard, physique, and vintage watch on his wrist are identical to mine. This memory is definitely a recent one by the looks of it.

Past Danny opens the text message and it's from my mom!

We just left Claire's house. Be home in half an hour.

Claire is a close family friend who my mom first met at her workplace many years ago. They often made plans together outside of work for lunches or dinners, especially on weekends. Since my mom used "we" in her message, it's implying that my dad is with her. I was probably driving by Brampton when my parents weren't home, so I must've decided to wait here in Gage Park until they returned.

Past Danny puts his phone away and picks up his notebook and pencil. He's meticulously working on a poem. Peri and I spend the next while quietly observing this process until he's finished. This poem is nothing close to the dreary one that I previously read in my bedroom. Instead, this one seems to be about nature and more fitting for the environment around us.

The old tree in the park is dying
It's lived a long life and it's not multiplying
It's witnessed kids climbing and toddlers crying
Cars passing by and airplanes flying
Its days are numbered and it's done trying

Every time you walk past a tree, it makes you believe
With its trunk, roots, branches, and leaves
It's a silent guardian that doesn't grieve
It provides us with comfort so we feel at ease
Watches the youth become adults who achieve
And one day find a job, move out, and leave

Life comes to an end for us all, it shouldn't be terrifying
Live it without regrets and it'll be satisfying
Treat all with respect and it'll be gratifying
Show the world your love and keep supplying
And don't forget about the old tree in the park that is dying

Love our Mother Earth, respect her as our home, and appreciate
all her natural beauty

The air
The breeze
The fire
The water
The rain
The snow
The dirt
The mud
The grass
The sand
The rocks
The warmth
The cold
The fog
The mist
The spring
The fall
The summer
The winter
The clouds

The moon
The sun
The sky
The animals
The plants
The trunks
The roots
The branches
The leaves
That belong to the old and dying trees

Past Danny draws a little tree at the bottom of the page before putting his pencil down.

"You have a talent," Peri says. "Don't let it go to waste."

"It was more of a hobby than anything else. I felt like there was always something to write about, even if it was about a plain old tree," I say.

I look around us and everything is completely normal and calm. It's a perfect summer evening with as gorgeous of a sunset as you could imagine. What could possibly go wrong here? I shouldn't be asking this question, as trouble will always find a way to present itself whenever and wherever it wants to.

Past Danny's phone abruptly starts ringing again, this time to the tune of an incoming call. He places his notebook and pencil down on the bench. He raises his phone to see who it is while Peri and I carefully monitor the scenario that's unfolding. There's no name from the caller as it seems to be an unknown number.

My heart skips a beat as Past Danny picks up.

"Hello? Yeah, that's me," Past Danny starts. "Wait… Where? When?" His tone becomes more anxious by the second. "I'm not far from there, I'm coming right now!"

Past Danny immediately gets up and throws everything into his satchel. He then starts sprinting toward the entrance of the park where the intersection is located. Peri and I follow closely behind him as my heart feels like it's about to burst out of my chest from the rapid beating.

Once he makes it out of the park, Past Danny frantically rushes to his car that's parked nearby on the street and sits in the driver's seat. It's the same car from the last memory, so I get into the backseat again with Peri beside me.

"What's going on?" I ask.

Peri remains silent and with each passing second, more fear builds within me.

Past Danny speeds the car through a few blocks, weaving in and out of traffic as fast as he can. Everything outside of the car is a jumbled blur. This is the opposite of the calm and peaceful drive through the forest with Jessica when I was able to see every detail of the landscape in motion.

Past Danny makes a hard left and then a right. His foot doesn't let off the pedal and his hands are gripping the steering wheel tightly. After a bit more speeding and a few more sharp turns, I notice a large intersection ahead of us that's entirely blocked off by yellow tape. Red and blue lights are flashing from multiple emergency vehicles parked around it.

Past Danny speeds the car one last time toward that area. The car comes to a screeching halt when we arrive behind the yellow tape. Past Danny viciously swings his door open and runs out of the car, leaving the key stuck in the ignition. Peri and I also get out to inspect this devastation before us.

There are two cars that appear damaged beyond repair, with metallic pieces and debris littered all over this intersection. The first car is in a stationary position while the other is completely upside down. Past Danny runs into the scene behind the yellow tape as I cautiously take a few steps forward. Before he's able to reach the flipped over car, a male police officer stops him in his tracks and restrains him from going any further.

I move closer to get a better look at what's going on and suddenly, I start hearing something that I don't comprehend right away. As soon as I realize it's Past Danny screaming at the top of his lungs, all is revealed and all is shattered.

"NO! MOM! DAD!"

His cries echo clearly and loudly enough for everyone at the scene to hear.

I instantly stagger down to the ground in front of Peri, as the most terrible memories come rushing back to my mind. Streams of tears start to run down my cheeks when I begin to remember everything that happened here. We're standing in what was the absolute worst day of my entire existence.

The car in front of me that's turned upside down is my parents' car. They're both inside of it with their seatbelts on, except I know that they're not moving or breathing anymore.

I feel my past self's suffering and it's beyond anything I've experienced thus far. The uncontrollable emotions are melting my brain, heart, and stomach. I'm being crushed from the inside out. I try to muster some words together as I'm in shock.

"I can't do this one. Please... Get me out of here right now," I say.

Peri grabs my arm and helps me back up from the ground.

"I'm here for you Danny," Peri says. "Whatever you're experiencing right now has already happened. This is only a memory."

Past Danny is still screaming in the background as the car doors are being cut open by a pair of firefighters. Paramedics are standing by, waiting to transport my parents' bodies away from the wreckage and into an ambulance.

My mind and body feel disoriented to the point where I can't even move. This moment is taking place almost two years after the last memory with Jessica on top of the peak. It's not in the far distant past, as all of this happened some time a few weeks ago.

"Peri I'm telling you... Please take me out. I'll endure any other memory but this one. I can't go through this trauma again," I say.

"The memory must run its course until the end," Peri says as he keeps his hand on my shoulder to help my balance. "Tell me what you're feeling Danny."

The pain from this memory sequence is so excruciating that I feel like my breath is being choked out of me. I watch the paramedics begin to move my parents' lifeless bodies away from their car on top of stretchers.

"They were only a few minutes away from home. They were literally *right there*," I say. "They didn't do anything wrong... They didn't deserve this."

"No, they didn't. But in the reality that you live in, this is the unfortunate scenario that *did* happen. It's how you choose to react to it that will define you," Peri says.

"I didn't even get to say goodbye…" I quietly mutter as I become lost in the moment.

When Past Danny sees mom and dad being carried to the ambulance, he becomes even more distraught from the situation. The same police officer uses both of his arms to forcefully move Past Danny aside so that he can get a hold of himself.

While that's happening in the background, my attention turns toward the other totalled car nearby, which is now a crumpled-up piece of metal. Paramedics are trying to revive the lone driver as he lays on the ground. My restored memory allows me to recall the fact that this is the person who was later identified as the sole reason behind this unnecessary accident.

I wipe away any lingering tears from my eyes and I feel the fury within me. I walk over to the driver, only to view his lifeless body and soulless eyes. The paramedics continue their efforts to save him, but I know that he won't make it out of here alive either. He's an ordinary middle-aged man and there's nothing special about him. However, I see him as the personification of death itself.

I remember that a day later, the police informed me that he had been heavily drinking and was out of his senses on the evening of the crash. He ran a red light at this intersection at a high speed and collided straight into my parents' car. This man's one bad decision led to destroying everything I had, including the last bits of my sanity.

I ball my hands up into fists, but I have nothing to say to this dead man laying in front of me. He was another individual within the swarm of billions that live on this planet. On any other day, he would've been a nobody to me. Now, it's his bloodied face that I'll always see in my mind when I think about my parents.

If it weren't his face, then it would've been someone else's. We can't choose our killers after all. There's pure hatred brewing within me that I don't know how to express. I continue to stare at this drunk driver's body until Peri approaches me from behind.

"Danny, it's okay. Let's move away from here," Peri says.

I stay put and don't reply to him.

"I'm here for you, take a deep breath," Peri says. "Come on over here."

Peri puts an arm around me and slowly guides me away from the wreckage.

"Let's sit down," Peri says. We approach a small bench beside a bus stop outside of the yellow tape. Peri sits me down before taking a seat right next to me.

We sit in silence as we observe the rest of the scene gradually come to an end. All the bodies have been urgently rushed away by paramedics. Past Danny leaves for the hospital as well, with the same police officer who was restraining him.

After a few minutes, all that's left is a few tow trucks and police officers who stay behind to clean up the area. Soon after that, the intersection will open back up again, and nobody will notice or care about the loss of life that occurred here. People will go about their days as usual, and it'll be another brief story for the next six o'clock news.

"Why'd this happen to them… Why'd this happen to me?" I ask, finally breaking the silence.

"It is said that everyone's path is preordained, already written since the day they're born. It's been called different things in different cultures, but here you call it *fate*," Peri says. "Just as we have no say about when or where we're born, we also don't have any say about when or where we'll naturally die."

"Whatever it is, my fate wants to kill me from the inside out. It's always been out to get me ever since I was a kid," I say. "All I ever wanted was to enjoy a normal life but to be honest, I don't even know what normal is anymore."

Peri scratches his beard as he watches a tow truck crew cleaning some debris in front of us.

"There's no real standard for what *normal* is… It's always been a matter of perspective," Peri says. "Your life, after all you've been through, may be repulsive to others who haven't been in your shoes, yet still seem exceptional to others who can't afford your shoes."

I sit in silence thinking about all the things I could've done to prevent this outcome from happening. Maybe I could've driven to Claire's house to see my parents instead of waiting at the park for them to come home. Perhaps I could've called my mom's phone and talked to her long enough to delay their car ride by a few minutes. Maybe I could've told my parents that I was swinging by the city earlier, so they would've stayed home instead. Or I could've bought my mom a newer and safer car that would've better absorbed the impact of the collision.

I'm thinking about a million different possibilities and scenarios where my parents may have lived to see another day. If only one of them had played out… but it's far too late now. I'm stuck in the one reality I never wished for.

"Is there such thing as a God?" I ask Peri.

"There's only that which we believe in our hearts," Peri says. "People believe in gravity. Even though they'll never see it with their own eyes, they'll always feel it around them. The same can be applied toward God… or used against him. There's no right or wrong answer."

"There can't be a God. If there was, then why has He always pushed me around like I don't belong in this world? Is it a test? Is He punishing me for something? Who have I ever hurt in my life? Forget about me, who did my mom ever hurt?" I ask.

"As I mentioned before, how you choose to react to adversity will define you for the rest of your life. If you want to blame God for this, then so be it… But you have to stay hopeful. You have to use every fiber in your body to make it through these tough times," Peri says.

I watch the last of the tow trucks drive off with the wrecked cars behind them. I'm aimlessly looking around at this intersection, knowing it will haunt me until the end of my days. The minutes seem to pass by like hours and I want to collapse at this point. The fog outside of this door has probably devoured the clearing by now.

With the tow trucks gone, the last of the police cruisers begin to trickle out of the scene as well. The last police officer walks around the area to remove the yellow tape and he allows the intersection to be open again. I stand up from the bench and look at Peri.

"What happens now? The memory's over. I did what you required of me. I lived through this nightmare again and I passed your trial," I say.

Peri remains sitting down and he doesn't say a word.

"What are you doing? Say something. Let's move on, I'm ready!" I say in a louder tone, trying to hide all the damage done within me. "Do your stupid snapping trick and change this environment now. Show me a positive memory that comes after this one, like you always do."

Peri looks down and lets out an audible sigh.

"Get up and let's get out of here man!" I yell. I yank Peri's arm in my attempt to get him off the bench but I'm unsuccessful.

"I don't want to stay here any longer," I plead. Fearing the worst, I start shaking Peri from his shoulder until he finally speaks.

"I'm sorry Danny," Peri says. "I can't change the environment this time… Not in this door."

My heart sinks to my stomach. What does he mean by that? When I need to escape from this unbearable torment more than ever, Peri's saying he can't do it.

In all the previous doors, I took comfort in knowing that there'd be a better time ahead to fall back on. There has to be something good that happened after this horrific day. There has to be *something* that revived my spirit.

"Peri stop messing around with me. We can go to the next memory now. Please…" I continue to plead.

"I can't do it Danny. It's not that I don't want to… but it's not possible," Peri says.

"Why? What's different this time?" I ask.

"There's no positive memory to go to," Peri admits. "It hasn't been made yet."

I sit back down on the bench beside him, filled with dread and defeat. I let out a sigh and look up at the sky.

"So, is that it? Nothing else can be done?" I ask, unsure of how to proceed with nowhere else left to go.

"I've yet to restore the final missing piece of your memory. This'll be hard for you, and you don't have to say anything. Just take a few minutes to collect your thoughts," Peri says.

I know he can see the pain in my swollen eyes and feel the suffering within my aching body.

"A big part of me doesn't want to know what happened after this day. If I fall into a dark place, will you help me out of it?" I ask, looking for any kind of reassurance.

"It's what I've been trying to do from the start," Peri replies. "Now look within yourself and face your inner demons once and for all. This is your final task," Peri says.

My greatest enemy on the battlefield has always been myself and my own mind. I hope it doesn't skewer me as soon as Peri provides me with the last piece of the puzzle.

"Do it," I say. I grip the bench tightly with both of my hands from the immense fear I feel.

"Good luck Danny," Peri says.

Peri holds his fingers right in front of my forehead and I close my eyes. A few seconds later, I hear his snap and it's as if my mind has been warped to another dimension. It's at that exact moment when the missing one percent of my memory finally returns to my severely broken mind.

I remember absolutely *everything*. I remember my childhood, my teenage years, my young adult years, my older years, and most importantly, I remember what happened in the past few weeks that led me here.

I was 31, soon to be 32 years old the day both of my parents died. I recall every single detail and event that occurred after that scarring incident. One man made the selfish decision to drink and drive on that summer evening, ultimately taking his own life along with the innocent lives of my mom and dad. I quickly realized that he had also claimed a fourth life… my own.

After my parents' funeral, I felt like there wasn't anything left for me in this world. At first, I thought about reaching out to my old friends like Sylvia, James, and Jessica to let them know what happened. I quickly rejected that idea because I just wanted to be alone without anyone else worrying about me.

I scattered my parents' ashes in the Credit River that would carry them onward and merge them with this vast land that they immigrated to all those many years ago. The weeks that followed thereafter were torture for me, as my life became utterly pointless and meaningless.

I became depressed beyond measure. I stopped going to work and I fell behind on my rent. I didn't message, call, or email anybody. I stayed cooped up inside of my old bedroom inside my parents' house with the curtains closed and no visitors or guests to divert my mind. I started to resent everything and everyone. I felt like I was thrown down to the absolute bottom pit of my mental health and I'd never be able to climb out of it. Food didn't taste the same anymore, the sunshine didn't warm my face, and entertainment didn't provide any escapism. There was nothing that excited me, nor did I look forward to anything in the future. Things that I once cherished and enjoyed, like reading, writing, exercising, music, and movies, were no longer important and I viewed them as unnecessary distractions.

I once tried searching what was happening to me and one of the associated terms that I found online was called "anhedonia," or in other words, the inability to experience any sense of pleasure in acts that once were. I became as nihilistic as a person could possibly be. Nothing but a jaded cynic who was a shadow of his former self. None of my gained knowledge about life over the years eased my suffering in any way. My moral principles crumbled and what little religious convictions I did have simply faded away. I was a walking blob of flesh with no soul, no heart, no confidence, no strength, no hope, and no purpose.

I viewed myself as an insignificant tiny ant, aimlessly wandering around a spinning rock in outer space. I felt completely non-existential, where none of my actions and words would ever matter to anyone or change anything. In fact, I didn't verbally speak for so long that I thought I lost the ability to do so.

I considered all possible angles and perspectives, eventually concluding that there could be no realistic solution to help me rid this everlasting pain. I knew that there'd be no more laughter or smiles coming from me, not even fake ones.

I may have been alive on the outside, but I was surely dead on the inside. I was nothing more than a moving corpse that needed to be laid to rest, like a spiritless zombie that was once human. I missed my mom more than anything and I cried so much that my tears eventually stopped flowing, like a dried-up well.

As much as I had disliked my dad throughout my entire life, we'd established some peace within the past few years. He'd been officially sober for over four years, and we were slowly mending our fractured relationship by openly communicating with each other. I could tell that my dad was in the process of becoming a changed husband and father, but that didn't seem to matter in the grand scheme of things. He was never truly able to wash away his regrets and atone for his sins, but at least he tried to make an effort. Despite our differences, he left this world as a more honourable and respectable man.

Once my parents were gone, I felt that I didn't have any other close relatives, friends, mentors, co-workers, or girlfriend to confide in and express my innermost feelings to. I was now the concrete definition of loneliness. I often revisited the idea of seeing a therapist, but I didn't have the energy within me to make a move and take any initiative whatsoever.

Eventually, there came a day when the absolute darkest of thoughts entered my mind, like a doctor preparing to cut off his patient's life support. I kept thinking that if I was going to live a miserable life like this every day for the next ten, twenty, or fifty years, then what was the point of it all? If I was to die in the end as a grumpy old man, then why shouldn't I fast forward to that moment now? Why should I merely delay the inevitable?

It's not like I'd be missing out on anything anyway. I'd seen everything I needed to see in the three decades I'd been alive. Millions of people have departed this world before me, and millions of people will depart long after me. Who remembers any of them?

I'd become nothing more than dust, which once belonged to a person who existed on this earth but whose memory would never be preserved by anyone. These deep questions and thoughts consumed my mind day in and day out. I was crawling down an endless rabbit hole that filled my soul with hopelessness, shame, and uncertainty.

My depression became so severe that I wanted to prematurely finish this game of chance that we call "life." I accepted my judgment, as I knew I'd have no one close to me that would mourn over my demise or be heartbroken from my permanent disappearance.

It was like the disease that I tried so hard to fight throughout my entire life had finally caught up to me for good. All those previous short-lived moments of happiness were minor treatments that aided in the remission against my hypothetical cancer. At the end of the day, they were only ever part of a temporary recovery before I would eventually succumb to my fate of an early departure.

The very thought of suicide had always been frightening to me because you never really think about it or see it up close, besides in dramatic movies. Yet here I was, thinking about all the many ways to do it and all the many places to do it at. I knew that I had complete control over its execution because there'd be no one to prevent me or talk me out of it.

The day that I decided to jump from a bridge was the day that my personal justifications far outweighed my hopeful possibilities of ever living a decent life again. I chose the Skyway Bridge over Lake Ontario because it was in a secluded location where no one could stop me even if they wanted to. This is the same bridge that I once looked at with pure joy when I was standing atop the peak with Jessica. Now, it would become the instrument of my own annihilation.

Thinking of Jessica, in almost two years that passed since our memorable trip to the peak, we only ever texted each other as friends. It never branched out into anything more romantic because of my constant reluctance to progress forward.

Jessica was patient with me and she made it clear that she wanted to understand my world, but I deliberately kept her sheltered from it. The reality is that I was never able to fully recover from Maya exploiting my trust, even though I knew Jessica was special and different from her. I kept my emotions bottled up inside of me for so long when I really should've spilled them all out to her.

My regrets didn't matter at that point, as I thought it was too late to pursue Jessica. As a departing gift, I planned to donate all my assets and personal belongings to the children's hospital. I thought they'd bring those innocent kids more pleasure and joy than they could ever do so for me again.

My plan had been finalized and I intended to go through with it. I would jump off the towering bridge and hope that the impact of the fall would end me right away. If it didn't, then I would drown because I never ended up learning how to swim.

I chose to do it in the middle of the night when there'd be much less traffic and people around who could possibly interfere. I had all the details worked out in my head like it was a necessary project that needed to be undertaken. I remember being afraid, but I also remember how desperate I was to escape this nightmare of a reality I was being forced to live.

The time came for me to follow through with my decision. I remember looking at my calendar on the wall that ominous night and it was coincidentally Friday the thirteenth. Not only that, but it was also the month of August. It was my 32nd birthday.

I wasn't much of a believer in superstitions, so I didn't think much of it and went ahead with my plan. I didn't leave any note for anyone, nor any pictures, videos, or anything else of value. I was wearing a dark grey t-shirt, blue jeans, and black shoes, which is the exact same outfit that I have on right now. Around 10:00 p.m. that night, I grabbed my wallet, phone, and car key before setting off for my final journey.

The drive was an hour away and I used the entire duration to remove any last-minute doubts that were slowly seeping into my mind.

Do I really want to do this? What would my mom say if she were here? Oh well, it's too late to think about that now… I'll be joining her soon.

I remember the radio wasn't playing and I sat in complete silence throughout the entire ride, most of it being on the highway. As I approached my final destination, I saw the dim lights on the bridge amid fog surrounding it underneath the moonlight.

I could've easily taken any of the upcoming exits to abort this mission if I wanted to, but I chose to push on. I saw my car's gas tank light switch on in the dashboard when I was a short distance away from the bridge, signaling that its fuel was almost empty. That may have been the final sign for me to take the next exit, fill up my gas tank, turn the car around, and stop this plan from proceeding any further. Instead, I simply viewed it as a metaphor for the energy left within me and I thought about how nothing would make me feel fulfilled again. I could fill my car up with gas, but I couldn't fill my soul up with happiness.

A few minutes of driving later and there it was. The daunting metallic structure stood strong a couple of hundred metres away from me. I took the last exit on the highway before the bridge, and I parked my car in an empty lot close by. I sat in silence for a few moments, still contemplating my decision and questioning what I was about to do. I could've driven home or slept in my car but instead, I thought enough was enough. I threw my wallet in the glove compartment, and I opened the door to get out.

I started walking up the ramp of the highway and I kept going until I was at the foot of the bridge. I paused again for some seconds as my mind was telling me to wait another day. I ignored this instinct and continued walking on the upward slope along the shoulder of the highway. I wouldn't stop now until I was at the very centre of this tall man-made structure.

It was a gloomy, windy, and foggy night on this Friday the thirteenth. Each car's headlights and backlights were a total blur as they passed by me. I had so many voices entering and exiting my mind that I thought I had officially gone crazy. I wanted to get rid of them once and for all.

When I made it to the centre of the bridge, I stood there for about ten minutes. I pulled out my phone and I foolishly expected to see hundreds of messages or phone calls telling me not to do it. Of course, there was no possibility of that considering I didn't tell anyone. I remember thinking that I could've at least left a small note behind for someone to find and read my explanation.

I briskly paced back and forth many times. I should've known to turn around and return home while I still had the chance, even after how far I'd come. I had enough opportunities to do so, but my mind was too far gone and enslaved to its dark side.

In my hesitation to quit, the moment finally came when the darkness within me prevailed over any light that was left. I gently climbed up on the railing of the bridge. I stood there for a few seconds as the wind blew in my face and I stared at the raging water below me. No one could possibly save me from this place now. No parents, no reliable friends, no companion. No one to tug me back from the edge. No one to pull me out of this literal and metaphorical darkness. It was time for the deed to be done. I looked up at the night sky and my last words were "forgive me." I then closed my eyes and plunged into the abyss below.

Something strange happened then that I didn't expect at all. As soon as my shoes left the railing and I was falling straight down toward my doom, I instantly regretted everything I did. I regretted my decision to jump, I regretted driving to the bridge, I regretted not turning back to go home, and I regretted having these miserable thoughts in the first place.

In those few seconds when my body was in a freefall, I wished so dearly that I could turn back time and go home. Like some cruel joke being played on me by nature, it took me jumping off a bridge to finally realize that I didn't want to die and needed a second chance at life. Within that lightning-fast moment, it was as if I'd been rehabilitated. I would've given anything to stay alive and avert this catastrophe, but it was far too late.

The very last thing I can squeeze out of my memory is hitting the water below me with such force that I lost consciousness... before I eventually awoke in shallow water by a shore.

I open my eyes, still sitting next to Peri on the bench by the bus stop. Cars are now rolling along in front of us where only recently, I saw my parents' lifeless bodies being carried away.

"I remember everything... I wanted to die but there was a split second where I wanted to live," I say to Peri.

"Well, which one is it?" Peri asks. "Now's your chance to decide that for good."

"I honestly don't know. Will I ever find happiness again?" I ask.

"That all depends on you. Happiness isn't something you can always find or chase," Peri replies. "If you want to doubt yourself and give up, we can remain sitting here... The fog will consume you and your life will come to an end, just as you intended. But if you can dig down and find even the smallest amount of hope left within you, it's still not too late to live a good life. It's entirely your decision to make, not mine. We're almost out of time, so it's now or never."

I keep seeing my parents and the drunk driver in my mind, no matter how hard I try to avoid it. It's impossible, like trying not to breathe. Millions of people suffer in this world every day, a place in which I feel I have no meaning or purpose. All my internal issues molded me into what I've become today.

An abusive father traumatizing me as a child, obsessing over school grades instead of learning, friends turning their backs on me, not being able to save Bella, drinking all my sorrows away, a fiancé cheating on me, and losing both my parents so suddenly without being able to say goodbye. Is it worth going back to all that?

There's no doubt that I've been broken beyond repair. I have problems entrenched within me that no one else will ever truly understand. If I do go back to my reality, there's a possibility that I won't be able to cope with what life throws at me and I'll only give up again. I can easily call it quits right here and now… It's what I wanted anyway.

With that being said, I remember making Peri a promise. I shook his hand on top of the peak and I promised him that I wouldn't give up. That I would try my best, despite what happens in my life. That I'd always keep my head up in the face of hardship and misfortune. I intend to keep this promise and hold true to my word.

As Peri awaits my decision, I turn to him and give him the biggest hug I can possibly muster. He's shown me the most wonderful memories from my past that I never would've thought about on my own. Memories that helped me realize how much I have to be thankful for.

I remember the happiness and enthusiasm that I felt in the arcade with my mom. I remember the valuable advice and wisdom that I listened to in Mr. Baker's guidance office. I remember the excitement and thrills from travelling with my friends, Sylvia and James. I remember the patience and acceptance that I learned from Annie at the children's hospital. I remember the adrenaline and determination that I fostered on my own within the gym. I remember the peace and pleasure that I enjoyed at the peak with Jessica. I have so many people left to talk to, so many more places to visit, and so much more beauty to experience in this world.

All the negative memories that preceded the good ones didn't break me down but instead, provided me with an opportunity to learn a valuable lesson from life and become stronger from the inside out. I miss my parents more than ever, but I know that I'll have to treat this particular memory as another one of those lessons because there's nothing that'll ever bring them back. Deep down within me, I know I have what it takes to move on and grow as a person. I know that I can try to create meaning and purpose within myself again.

"Thank you for saving me... I want to live... I need a second chance more than anything," I say to Peri with tears in my eyes.

I'm desperately clinging on to him, something I never imagined doing when I first met him. This stranger who became my mentor was now my friend.

"Thank you for showing me what it means to be human," I say.

"You've done well," Peri says with an arm around me. "I'm proud of you Danny, and I'm certain your parents are too."

I feel reassured as my confidence and hope are slowly returning to me by driving out all the deeply rooted pessimism.

"Let's get you out of here now," Peri says as he stands up. "You've passed your trial. You don't belong here after all."

"There's no exit door or any other portal with the white light. How are we supposed to leave?" I ask while also standing up.

"Oh, like this," Peri says with a smirk.

He snaps his fingers and a tiny black sphere, no bigger than the size of a marble, is formed on the very tip of his finger. It seems harmless at first, until everything around us begins to move toward this one point. It doesn't take long for me to realize that this entire environment is beginning to collapse inward on itself. This sphere grows larger with each passing second, resembling an expanding black hole that's forcibly drawing everything into it.

Besides me and Peri, every object within the environment, no matter how big or small, is being pulled into the centre of this singularity. The roads, the cars, the streetlights, the pedestrians, the trees, and the bench that we were sitting on are quickly disappearing from my sight. Everything is being warped right into the middle of this strange darkness that Peri has created, as if he's showing me one last magical spectacle.

Eventually, when there's not a single remnant left of the environment, Peri and I start to get sucked into this pitch-black abyss as well. There's no bright, warm, comfortable white light where we're headed but whatever it takes to leave, I'm all for it.

As we enter this spontaneous portal, I feel colder than ever before. This is probably what the lake felt like after I had plunged into it from the bridge. I begin to shiver and decide to close my eyes, hoping for whatever's happening to conclude as soon as possible.

The discomfort doesn't last long as the chills instantly withdraw, and I feel my body in a sudden freefall. I land on the ground about a metre below me, where Peri is already standing. He quickly helps me up by grabbing my arm.

"Up you get," Peri says.

I look around the claustrophobic area as the deadly fog is closing in on us. There are no more doors left, as the seventh and final one has vanished. Since we've been gone, the fog has moved so close that I must have only a few minutes left before it touches me. The crows are flying right above my head like they're about to swoop down at any second and start picking my flesh apart.

"How'd you do that?" I ask Peri. "I thought you said that you were only able to change the environments within the doors, not get us out of them!"

Peri chuckles and takes a few steps away from me. He aims both of his hands down at the ground with his fingers spaced apart, almost as if he's about to conjure a spell. Before anything happens, he speaks to me, perhaps for the last time before I can leave.

"Danny, who do you think designed this place? The memories were yours but the doors and everything else here is mine," Peri says.

"What do you mean? What about your master? The one who sent you to help me?" I ask.

"I should've told you this earlier, but I'm not a messenger for anyone. I serve no master. It was me who was testing you all along. I needed to see if you had the will to persevere, change your mindset, and reignite your desire to live," Peri says.

I stare at Peri with my mouth wide open, who seems to have been someone else this whole time.

"If you had failed your trial, I would've ferried you off to the next world. You proved me wrong by succeeding," Peri says.

He then uses his hands to summon a structure that erupts from beneath us. It's emerging high above the ground and appears to be a stone archway, right in between me and Peri. We look at each other from the open gap inside as the fog draws closer from every direction.

Peri walks up to the centre of the archway, and he extends his hand through it.

"It's not your time yet, but I'll see you again one day. Until then, go be free, live your life to its fullest, and make more positive memories to overcome your grief… You still have much to live for."

Peri's words hit me like a thunderstorm as this is the most information he's revealed since we met. I remain silent and I walk up to the archway as Peri nods in approval. The fog is only a few metres away now and the crows are cawing louder than ever before.

I shake Peri's hand with confidence and look him right in the eyes to solidify the end of our bittersweet journey.

"Thank you for everything you've done. I'll uphold the promise I made to you," I say.

Peri smiles and takes a few steps back again. He snaps his fingers aimed toward the stone archway.

I take a few steps back myself with caution. My back is up against the wall of fog now, and I can feel it eagerly trying to grasp my soul from behind. Another portal opens within the stone archway, which appears to be much calmer this time around.

"Walk through the archway and go back to your world before it's too late Danny!" Peri shouts. His back is also against the fog, which continues to close in on us.

The portal is emitting a subtle white light, but it's transparent enough for me to see Peri on the other side. I walk up to the portal and stop myself right in front of it. Before I walk through and depart from this place, I need to clear something up.

"Who are you?" I ask. This burning question has irked my curiosity from the beginning.

Peri starts to laugh out loud and I'm sure that's his final answer. Oh well, at least I tried. As I'm about to take my first step into the portal, Peri shouts something over to me.

"Your answer has always been right in front of you. Farewell Danny and good luck!" Peri yells.

Peri then takes his knife out from his back pocket, which I haven't seen since he first approached me on the shore. He then takes a step back into the dense fog and it completely devours him from top to bottom.

I suppose that's the end of that, as I have nothing else left to do or say but to walk through the portal. I don't know what he meant, but Peri always did have a way with his words.

I feel the fog breathing down my neck behind me, mere seconds away now. The portal is right in front of my eyes… It's now or never.

I look through the transparent portal to the other side one last time and to my surprise, I notice something that resembles alphabetical letters. They're appearing one at a time within the thick fog where Peri just disappeared. I squint my eyes to get a better look. I can't see Peri but I'm able to make out the letters he's writing with the tip of his knife, as if he's showing me another one of his tricks.

They're a bit hazy but the letters seem to form two distinct words, one on top of the other.

PERI

GRAMER

What happens next frightens me at first but makes me chuckle the very next second as if I should've known this all along. The letters in the fog have been rearranged to spell something else.

GRIM

REAPER

So, it was an anagram this whole time. Before I can dwell on this revelation any further, the end has come.

The fog places its haunted hands on my shoulders from behind while all the crows above fly down toward my head at once. Right before they can claim me and prevent me from returning to my reality, I step forward into the portal.

Inside of it, a glimmering light shines brightly and I become unaware of my surroundings. The piercing light consumes my body and I surrender myself to its warm embrace. I close my eyes and tell myself that it'll all be over soon. I hope with all my heart that I make it out of here alive and that the worst is truly behind me. I no longer feel the clutches of the fog or hear the cawing of the crows. It's only me, alone with my thoughts and memories. I'm floating away and being reborn within this gentle, calming light.

It's been so long since I've rested. Maybe I can finally take a break now... Maybe I can finally sleep for a while.

THE MARATHON

I awaken with light surrounding me. My body is sprawled out on solid ground. The first thing I see is sand, which covers half of my face, and the first sound I hear is water that softly moves forward before receding.

I slowly pick myself up from the ground and shake myself as clean as I can. The sun is rising in the horizon and its rays paint the sky with a beautiful shade of orange. I look down and empty my pockets. I have my car key and my phone, which still isn't working. I notice that the watch on my wrist is working again though. Its second hand is ticking once more as if it's come back to life.

I recognize where I am. It's the same shore I washed up on when my memory was wiped. This is where I met Peri for the first time and took my first steps in the direction of the forest. It's the same place but much has changed now.

There's not a single crow flying above the treetops, no approaching fog to worry about, no more eeriness to the atmosphere, and most of all, no more darkness. Before I do anything at all, I need to know what's in the forest in front of me. Did I really experience everything that happened within it?

I begin walking toward the forest in my hope to confirm the existence of the magical clearing. I leave the shore and step past the boundary of dense trees. I carefully move deeper into the forest, walking the exact same path that I previously did.

After some minutes of hiking and weaving my way around the infinite trees, I think I see something a few steps away. There's a clearing that stands out from the rest of the forest. I walk up to it and believe that this is the same clearing where I underwent my trial. There's nothing within it besides some small plants, shrubs, and grass. It's just a simple area where trees don't grow as much as the rest of the forest.

I decide to walk right into the middle of it where I concluded my journey of a lifetime. There's complete silence around me. This seems to be the place that broke me down and tore me apart, but somehow put me back together with more strength and hope than ever before. I'm standing where the last portal was created, the one that brought me back here. It's nothing more than empty ground now without anything magical about it.

I get down on one knee and place my right palm on the ground, feeling every tiny blade of grass between my fingers. I feel a slight breeze of wind that strikes my face. I'll take it as a sign to stop lingering here and move on. The question is what do I do and where do I go now? I pause for a moment and contemplate the first thing that I should do if this is indeed my second chance at life. I think I know what it is.

I get up, turn around, and start running all the way back to where I came from. I arrive at the shore and start looking for a possible exit. I don't see any options, so I continue running upward along the shore that parallels the edge of the forest. I don't stop for any breaks and even when I run out of breath, I keep going.

I push forward with the sandy shore below me, the calming water on my left, and the dense forest on my right. With each stride that I take, I'm reinvigorated with the confidence surging throughout my bones. I'm thankful for each breath I take and being able to experience my beautiful surroundings, as if I was only born a few minutes ago.

Everything feels brand new like I have a fresh pair of lenses over my eyes. I was a blank canvas when I lost all my memories, and I was enlightened when I gained all of them back. The truth is that this canvas has much more room to expand with the promising future that lays ahead of me.

I keep running with determination as the minutes pass by. As the shore begins to veer toward my right-hand side, I hear a different sound besides water. It's the sound of moving cars somewhere out in front of me and above me.

I run onward along the shore until I see where most of those cars are and where they're coming from. It's the Skyway Bridge. Is this structure still the instrument of my doom or is it now the reason for my salvation? I try not to ponder too much about the deep questions and focus on moving ahead. I run along the shore until I see a pathway behind a yellow gate that may be the best way out of here. I sprint toward the yellow gate and jump over it as if I'm competing for a gold medal. My strides get bigger as I make my way up this path that eventually connects me to the main road.

Once I reach this road with the passing cars, I finally take a break to catch my breath. The Skyway Bridge is a short distance away from me. I don't pay any attention to it because the view in front of me is like a dream.

Here I am, standing by the roadside with a stunning orange sunrise that highlights all of Lake Ontario. This is the type of view to make you really appreciate being alive to witness it. This whole vista with the sunrise and the bridge represents a contrast between life and death for me.

I'm still not sure if whatever happened in the forest clearing was real or an illusion. Was there such a place with dangerous fog, frightening crows, magical doors, and the Grim Reaper himself? Or did I simply survive the fall from the bridge and lose consciousness until now? Maybe I saw my life flashing in front of my eyes before I really died and miraculously came back to life?

I may never know the actual truth about what I experienced. Some things are better left unexplained. I doubt anyone would believe me if I tried elaborating on any of these theories anyway, but I personally choose to stick with the first one. I do believe that there was someone out there for me in my bleakest moment. Someone who helped me out of the darkness, saved me from my own destruction, and rewarded me with a valuable second chance.

I take a deep breath and I begin to run in the direction of the bridge. I don't know how much time has passed but my car may still be parked close by. I don't know if I've been missing for one night or ten. Either way, it doesn't matter to me and I continue running. The slope gradually increases so I push harder with each step that I take. I view this as my last hurdle before I can sit down and reminisce about all the craziness I've been through. I run as fast as my legs can go until I reach the exact midway point of the bridge.

I stop here to look out toward the lake again. This is the same spot I jumped on that horrible night and the same spot I wished that I could take it back the second I began to fall. My wish somehow came true and I'm standing here as a testament for my will to survive. I'm thankful to be able to see another day. If only Peri, or "Grim" if I want to be technical about it, could see me now.

I'm off again as I dash toward the downward slope of the bridge. The last hurdle is behind me, and the worst seems to be behind me as well. I make it to the foot of the bridge and take the first exit. I don't know when I'll be back here again, but I'll bet that it won't be any time soon. I slow my pace down and jog on the sidewalk to the parking lot, where my car should be awaiting my arrival.

There's an elderly gentleman walking in my direction on the same sidewalk, so I move over before I pass him.

"Good morning!" I say as I approach him.

"Hello! Great morning for a jog," the old man replies with a beaming smile.

"Yes it is, take care!" I say as I pass him.

"Enjoy your day young man!" the old man shouts behind me.

I'm filled to the brim with happiness from this brief interaction with that stranger. I continue to jog until I see the parking lot that I've been using all my strength to get to. It resembles the finish line for this marathon that began from the centre of the clearing in the forest.

Come to think of it, a marathon of life is what everyone in this world is running. It's a marathon filled with all the highs and lows of everyday life that are simply unavoidable. Joy, suffering, excitement, misery, satisfaction, and disappointment. Each person is attached to this marathon with their own unique pace from how they react to their individual highs and lows. Some are slow, some are fast, some are right in the middle, and some are quitters. I was one of the quitters that gave up on the marathon without considering all the rewards I had gained since starting it. Now that I've been given a chance to pick up where I left off, I intend to make the most of it with each new day that I live.

I now realize that it's alright to experience occasional setbacks and that it's better to view them as a challenge for motivating myself to overcome them. What matters most is that I keep my head held high throughout those temporary difficulties and press on without falling into despair again. My marathon of life will continue because I know I have what it takes to run it, enjoy it, and see it through to the very end.

At last, I've made it to my car that's in the same spot where I left it. I take my key out of my pocket and unlock the door. I sit down behind the steering wheel, recline my seat all the way back, and sit alone in silence. I'm sure it'll take me months, if not years, to process what happened and what I went through. Maybe the less I think about it, the better off I'll be. Besides, what I choose to do going forward is more important than fixating on anything from the past. I turn the radio on to deflect my thoughts for a moment.

"…we'll be seeing a high of 31 and a low of 19 at night. It's currently 22 outside with beautiful conditions for your morning. So far, a great start to the weekend! It's 6:50 a.m. on Saturday, August 14th. Stay tuned as we discuss business when we return…"

I turn the radio off and revert to the silence. My birthday has passed, and I've only been gone for a few hours when it felt like years. With that being established, I recline my seat forward, turn the key in the ignition, and feel the car vibrate. I put it in drive and speed toward the nearby highway ramp.

As the car enters the highway, I feel comfort in driving away from this area where I've overstayed my welcome. This all still feels surreal to me, so I continue to sit in silence for the next hour.

As my trip is almost at an end, I direct my attention to some of the buildings that quickly pass by alongside the highway. I first happen to notice a big arcade with a go-karting track outside of it to my left.

"Thank you, mom," I say out loud.

I then see an unknown public school with a bright green football field on my right.

"Thank you, Mr. Baker."

The crowded downtown core of Toronto is far off in the distance in front of me, looking like a mini version of New York City.

"Thank you, Sylvia and James."

That's also where the children's hospital is located, about ten minutes away from the CN Tower.

"Thank you, Annie."

There's a huge gym coming up on my left where people are getting their early morning workouts in.

"Thank you me," I say before chuckling, knowing that I'll be back in the gym again as soon as tomorrow.

The Skyway Bridge is way behind me and I can't see it anymore, but that doesn't mean I'll ever forget what happened there.

"Thank you, Peri."

I take a specific exit off the highway and continue to drive around a few more streets until I'm a short distance away from my destination. I hope this goes alright and whatever happens, happens. Regardless, my life has begun anew and after what I've been through, I don't think there's anything that could break me down so soon again.

I finally reach the street I intended to travel to. My heart begins to beat out of my chest, but I know this is something that can't wait. I park alongside the curb outside of a townhouse and I remain in my car.

I open the glove compartment to get out a pen and notebook that I always kept inside. Whenever I had any thoughts for a new poem, I had the urge to write them down on paper before they slipped my mind. As I browse through my notebook, I glance at the page on which I last wrote on. It's a poem I had completed a few days before I jumped off the bridge.

Depression is when you're colourblind in a world where you're constantly being told how colourful it is…

I stop after the first line and let out a sigh. I skip some lines down without reading everything in between.

Depression is when you're living in a body that's fighting to survive with a mind that has already surrendered…

I choose not to read any further. The dark tone is consistent throughout this poem, which isn't what my renewed mindset needs anymore.

Like venom that needs to be extracted, I tear out the entire page and toss it into the glove compartment. I flip over to a blank page and with my pen, I begin scribbling down the first lines of something new.

The toughest challenges in life require a courageous fight

Whenever there is darkness of night, remember what follows is light

I think about how far I've come since childhood. I'll try not to let anything break me down anymore. Once you've been at the bottom of the pit, the only direction left to go is up. I'll always remember that good times will eventually follow any bad times, even if they're few and far between. After all, you can't rise from the ashes unless you've burned in fire first. You only have one life to live and it's entirely up to you to make the most of it, despite any of the dreadful cards you've been dealt.

You can choose to mold yourself with confidence and hope, or you can let the world beat you down with negativity until you're pushed over the edge. It's an endless mind game that can either make or break you. If the dark and depressing thoughts within your mind can be conquered, nothing can hold you back from attaining the happiness that you deserve.

I place my notebook and pen back into the glove compartment. I'll pick up on this new poem some other time. Right now, there's something more important to attend to that's long overdue. With my restored outlook on life, I get out of my car and take a deep breath.

I start walking toward the townhouse as the sky is now a lovely shade of blue. I approach a wooden door that has a brass doorknob attached to it. I knock on the door three times and patiently wait for a response. A few seconds later, the knob begins to turn before the door is opened wide.

"Danny!?" she excitedly says with a huge smile on her face. She takes a step outside of her door, standing in her light blue pyjamas and a white t-shirt. Her dark hair is pulled back in a ponytail and her face lights up my soul like a thousand suns. I haven't seen anyone more beautiful in my life.

"Jessica… Thank you," I say to her before I embrace her. She places her arms around me in return, as if no amount of time has passed since we last saw each other.

"For what? It took you long enough to stop by," Jessica says as she grips me tighter.

"More than you'll ever know," I reply.

Our hug lasts for what seems like an eternity. There's no place else I'd rather be in the world right now than in her arms. She's the one for me, and always has been since I first met her all those years ago. I believe I can trust her with all my heart and rely on her no matter what the future holds.

"I tried reaching out to you in the past few weeks. You never returned any of my calls or texts," Jessica says.

"I'm sorry for pushing you away like that. It won't happen again Jessica," I say.

"It better not," she whispers back. "I really missed you."

I should've done this months ago. I've been distracted long enough. It's my turn to make things right and this is where I start. There's nothing more I want than to be with her forever.

We finally lower our arms and stare into each other's eyes.

"Well, you look like you could use some breakfast! I was just about to have some cereal, come on in Danny," Jessica says with a smile that doesn't fade. She kindly holds her door open for me.

I remember my parents once more, as well as the old man who called himself Peri Gramer. I hope that he's looking over me now because I wouldn't be here without him.

Thank you for this second chance. I will keep the promise I made to you.

I step forth into the doorframe with my head up and Jessica follows me in, gently closing the door behind her.

ACKNOWLEDGEMENTS

I'd like to thank the following people for helping me get this far and always supporting me no matter what I pursue.

My mother, Mandeep, showed me how to believe in myself and helped me understand the rewards that stem from compassion, respect, and honesty.

My father, Jatinder, taught me the value of working hard and staying humble while being the best role model a son could ever ask for.

My brother, Manveer, had my back throughout our craziest moments since we were kids and I'm glad that our friendly rivalry continues as we're adults.

My grandparents, Parminder, Pritam, Jagdish, and Karnail departed from this world far too soon but their influences will always be a part of my identity.

My best friend, Kriti, pulled me out of the darkness and brought me back to the light whenever I was at my lowest points on this roller coaster of life.

I couldn't ask for a better group of people to encourage me and I hope that I've made you all proud with this achievement. All of you have inspired me to become the man that I am today, and I'll remain thankful for your guidance until the end of my days.

ABOUT THE AUTHOR

Jaskaran Chahal was born in the city of Mississauga, Canada, and raised in the city of Brampton.

As a teenager, he started to develop an interest in writing from taking high school courses related to history, law, politics, religion, and philosophy.

Jaskaran Chahal loves great storytelling, whether it's found within a book, film, video game, or song. His favourite story since childhood has been The Lord of the Rings.

Jaskaran's academic achievements include an Honours Bachelor of Arts degree from the University of Toronto, as well as a Bachelor of Education degree and a Master of Education degree from York University.

If you would like to say hello or have a conversation about Seven Doors to Salvation, you can reach out to him through his blog site at: https://jazzywritesblog.com/

www.ingramcontent.com/pod-product-compliance
Lightning Source LLC
Chambersburg PA
CBHW021130190726
48288CB00008B/2591